ALIBI FOR INSPECTOR WEST
(Formerly *ALIBI*)

Sensing rather than hearing movement, he half-turned,
caught sight of the dark, shiny hair of a man bent low
behind him. Then he felt hands thump against his shoulders
and went hurtling forward, banging his forehead against
the door. It swung open, and he fell headlong into the
room. His head smacked against the floor, nearly stunning
him, but he was aware of hands gripping his wrists and
lifting his legs up, then pushing him to one side. The next
moment he was kicked savagely in the ribs, then the door
slammed and the light went out. He was alone, in
darkness, gasping for breath.
Gasping.
He was aware of many things—mostly fear.

John Creasey's books have sold nearly a hundred
million copies and have been translated into 28 languages.
Born in 1908, John Creasey has a home in Arizona,
U.S.A., since more of his books sell in the United States
than in any other country. He also has his home in
Wiltshire, England, and he virtually commutes between the
two.
He has travelled extensively, and is very interested in
politics. He is founder of All Party Alliance and has fought
four elections for this movement, advocating government
by the best men from all parties and independents.
Married three times, he has three sons.

Also by the same author

Strike for Death
Murder London—Miami
Inspector West Kicks Off
Send Inspector West
Policeman's Dread
Inspector West At Home
Inspector West Cries Wolf

and available in Coronet Books

Alibi for Inspector West
(Formerly *Alibi*)

John Creasey

CORONET BOOKS
Hodder Paperbacks Ltd., London

Printed in Great Britain
for Coronet Books, Hodder Paperbacks Ltd.,
St Paul's House, Warwick Lane, London, E.C.4,
by Richard Clay (The Chaucer Press), Ltd.,
Bungay, Suffolk

ISBN 0 340 17320 3

CONTENTS

Chapter One

FIRST APPEARANCE

'And is the accused represented in court?' asked Charles Gunn.

He did not think for one moment that the slender young man standing in the dock would have a lawyer here; he didn't appear to have two pennies to rub together. Yet he had a scrubbed look, and was clean-shaven and short-haired. No one of his age, and he must be in his middle twenties, should have those sunken cheeks and eyes so vividly bright in their deep, dark sockets. He stood upright and very still, looking straight at Gunn, the magistrate on duty that morning.

'No,' he said, clearly.

Farriman, the fussy little, prim little, knowing little magistrates' clerk, fussed with papers and spoke as if he had not heard the prisoner's answer.

'No sir, he's not represented. Perhaps you could suggest legal aid.'

'Does the accused plead guilty or not guilty?' Gunn asked. He never ceased to be slightly exasperated by the clerk, but seldom showed it.

Again the prisoner answered very clearly.

'Not guilty, sir.'

Gunn looked at the young man, wondering what were the events that had led up to the act of violence that had brought him here. This had all the appearances of a straightforward and simple case; and a grave one. The prisoner was accused of 'hitting a man over the head with a musical instrument, to wit, an electric guitar, with intent to cause grievous bodily harm'. 'Grievous bodily harm' could bring life imprisonment, but was likely to be seven to ten years, unless the man who had been attacked died.

Gunn brought himself up sharply. He was thinking in terms of the accused's guilt, and that was both wrong and unusual. All he had heard so far was the evidence of arrest and the charge. He was very conscious of that direct gaze; but he had long since learned, however keen his concentration on the man in the dock, to be aware of the rest of the court. Any unusual movement, while seldom distracting him, was carefully noted; and he noted now the unexpected appearance of a latecomer. This latecomer, tall, lean, strong-looking and quite unusually handsome, gave a respectful nod to the bench—to Gunn —and joined the grey-haired Chief Inspector of the Metropolitan Police, who had made the formal charge.

'I wonder what's brought West,' Gunn remarked to himself. And, seeing the prisoner's gaze flicker blankly for a moment, 'Rapelli doesn't recognise him.'

The two senior policemen were whispering, the three newspapermen in the Press Box now seemed much more interested in West than in anything else, the court officials, including the two wardens with Rapelli, all watched West. That wasn't really surprising. Chief Superintendent Roger 'Handsome' West was probably the best-known policeman in England, with the possible exception of the commander of the Criminal Investigation Department. Moreover, he attracted publicity as a candle attracts moths. His looks; his flair for detection; his persistence and thoroughness and—not least—the countless examples of his unflinching physical courage, all contributed to his reputation. He seldom came to court, and Gunn could not remember him coming to this one except on a major case.

So, why was he here this morning? Why should the apparently impetuous crime, the result of a fight between two young men, bring this senior policeman whose desk must be covered with details of investigations into major crimes?

The grey-haired Chief Inspector, Leeminster, turned away from West, who sat back on the police bench and crossed his legs. He did no more than glance at the man in the dock.

All of this had taken only a few seconds yet it had brought a noticeable lull, creating a mood almost of suspense. This was heightened as Leeminster neared the bench, and as the door to the public benches opened and a young woman came in. On that instant, two things happened at once. Charles Gunn saw West glance very appraisingly at the girl. And the three reporters moved, putting their heads together as if as impressed by this arrival as by West's.

'What is it? What is it?' Farriman the magistrates' clerk asked Leeminster.

'The police ask for a remand in custody,' said Leeminster.

Of course they did on such a charge, thought Gunn, even more puzzled. Leeminster, obviously prompted by West, had repeated that request quickly.

The girl was passing the public benches and approaching those where the police and the solicitors and officials sat. She was very striking-looking, her slender figure making her appear taller than in fact she was, and wore an olive green suede suit and tightly fitting hat, which practically covered her short, chestnut-brown hair. She glanced coldly at West, and Gunn felt sure the two had met before. He was mildly amused, for West had the reputation of being a ladies' man.

The girl came straight up to the bench. The prisoner seemed to shape his lips to speak and his grip on the rail became very tight. West moved back in his seat—amused? wondered Gunn; or resigned?

Farriman, who had also been distracted, had taken his time writing down the police request. Now, pretending not to notice the girl, he said, 'The police request a remand in custody, sir. The usual period is eight days.' Farriman must have irritated a dozen magistrates by that piece of gratuitous information.

'I would be grateful for a hearing now, your honour,' the girl said clearly.

Gunn realised that she was nervous. The formal words, the over-precise enunciation, the huskiness of her voice, all told him that. But at close quarters she was astonishing-looking, with a superb, near-olive coloured complexion, beautiful brown eyes, a short, narrow-tipped nose, bow-shaped lips and a pointed chin. Her face was unusually narrow, which somehow made her looks more striking.

'What qualification have you to address the court?' demanded Farriman. He would never learn to allow the man on the bench to give a lead as to his own attitude.

'I am a solicitor,' she stated, her voice still husky, 'and I would like to represent the accused.'

'The prisoner has already pleaded,' Farriman fussed, and at last looked up at Gunn. He could only see Gunn's head and shoulders, and Gunn could only see a foreshortened view of his grey hair with the pink bald patch, his pince-nez on a flabby nose.

'He pleaded not guilty,' Gunn said mildly.

'I should think so,' said the girl, with greater assurance. 'I think—'

'Please, please,' interrupted Farriman. 'If the bench would like to hear you then will you please—' He broke off.

'Do you wish to be represented by this young lady?' Gunn asked Rapelli.

Rapelli moistened his lips and said something.

'Speak up, speak up!' Farriman urged.

Gunn opened his mouth, on the verge of angry reproof, checked himself, scribbled *'leave this to me'* on a slip of paper and leaned forward and handed it down to Farriman who adjusted his pince-nez, frowned, read and read again. There was a fresh tension in the court, and now everyone was watching Rapelli closely.

'Let me ask you another question,' Gunn said to the accused. 'Do you know this young lady?' He smiled down at the girl. 'Perhaps you will turn round so that the accused may see you.'

She narrowed her eyes in a frown which brought a deep groove between her eyes, then turned abruptly, and said, 'We know each other very well. Don't we, Mario?'

The young man moved his lips, and admitted 'Yes.'

'Do you wish to be represented by her?' Gunn asked again. 'You may be, and I am quite prepared to allow you time for discussion in private.'

Farriman wriggled in disapproval. Everyone, including Roger West, was staring at the couple. There was a facial similarity between them and their lean, spare figures made them look as if they might be brother and sister.

'I would like her to represent me,' Rapelli said at last; and he closed his eyes.

'Very well. If you will give the Clerk your name and qualifications, we may proceed,' said Gunn.

In a clear voice, she gave her name: Rachel Warrender. She was a junior partner in the firm of Warrender, Clansel and Warrender, of Lincoln's Inn. She asked if she could consult with her client while he was in the dock, having no wish to take up the court's time. She went up to Rapelli, and placed a hand on the rail, obviously for no purpose but to touch his. Only the warders could hear what they said, but it was obvious that Rapelli spoke in little more than monosyllables.

At last, Rachel Warrender turned and looked at Chief Inspector Leeminster. Leeminster had not moved from the time she had arrived, and in some way—a way which made him invaluable as a detective—he seemed to have faded into the background. Only now did anyone appear to notice him.

'I confirm my client's plea of not guilty,' she said, 'and I would like to ask for a dismissal of the charge, which has no justification whatsoever.'

'Oh,' said Gunn, and pursed his lips. 'Dismissal.' If this young woman persisted in her request then he would have to decide how to respond: order an eight day remand, the normal way, without taking evidence; or accept evidence now, which he could by stretching a point. If he did this the court would have to call police and other witnesses, hear much more than the simple evidence of arrest already given. It could take an hour; several hours, perhaps. Well, this was his job and time wasn't vital; but there were at least six other cases waiting, each of them likely to be one for summary justice. He might have to adjourn and make arrangements for another magistrate to take the waiting cases.

'The police submit that they will need at least six or seven days in which to complete their enquiries,' Leeminster stated. 'We respectfully repeat our application for a remand in custody, your honour.'

'The enquiries can be completed in this court, in ten minutes,' stated Rachel Warrender with stinging acerbity.

'I think I can satisfy the court that there is no case to answer.'

'Do you propose to bring witnesses?' asked Gunn.

'Yes, sir. Three witnesses who will state—'

'*Really!*' Farriman exploded. 'We cannot be told in advance what witnesses will state.'

'We can and should be told in advance what the accused's representative expects to establish,' Gunn said urbanely. 'What do you hope to establish, Miss Warrender?'

'That my client could not have committed the crime he is accused of because he was at least six miles away from the place where it was committed,' stated Rachel. She spoke much more clearly now, her voice was firmer and her manner assured. She glanced at Farriman, as if to say: I know what I'm doing as well as you.

Gunn said, 'And what have the police to say?'

'The police are quite satisfied that they can prove the charge,' Leeminster declared with equal firmness.

'And can you bring witnesses?'

'We can, sir, in due course.'

Gunn contemplated them both, aware of West watching him intently, and sensed that, for a reason which he couldn't yet see, this was an important issue for the police. There was another point: the prosecution, in this case the police, could not be denied a remand to enquire into an alibi. If she were a good lawyer, the young woman certainly knew that as well as the police. So they were deliberately sparring, as if each was anxious to find out how far the other would go.

So Rapelli would have to be remanded. The only question was whether it should be on bail or in custody.

'How long do you say it will take the police to prepare their case?' he asked.

'About a week, sir,' Leeminster repeated.

'I can submit the defence now,' said Rachel Warrender. 'I have my witnesses outside the courtroom.' She really was pushing hard, as if hoping that the police would yield, even withdraw the case, or at least withdraw their opposition to bail. When Gunn didn't respond she went on with a touch of impatience, 'If there are three witnesses who can state categorically that my client could not possibly have committed the crime since he was in another place at the time the crime was committed, surely that would justify a dismissal, your worship.'

Leeminster kept silent, leaving this to the court.

'No,' said Gunn, after a brief pause. 'As it is a defence of alibi, the police will have every right to insist on a remand. When can you produce your witness, Chief Inspector?'

'I would hope within the week, sir, but I cannot say for certain until we have completed our enquiries.'

'And you still ask for a remand in custody?'

'We do, sir.'

'On what grounds?'

'That the accused's life could be in jeopardy, or alternatively that he could leave the country,' Leeminster stated.

Gunn did not speak immediately, but pursed his lips, leaned back in the beautifully carved oak chair and looked up at the intricately decorated ceiling. He was aware of the way everyone looked at him, knew that his decision would be as important to the police as to the accused and his lawyer. He, Charles Gunn, was suddenly and unexpectedly presented with a very difficult problem. He was quite sure that the police would not have asked for custody on any grounds unless they were convinced of the need, and the decision rested solely on him. With Farriman, stickler for the rule and regulation, breathing stertorously below him, West, the prisoner and this young woman staring at him intently, he felt very much on the spot.

Suddenly, he leaned forward.

'Mr. Farriman—'

Farriman climbed slowly, arthritis-bound, from his chair, and his head and shoulders appeared over the front of the bench. He kept his voice low so that no one else could hear.

'Yes, your honour?'

'Is there any provision, Mr. Farriman, for hearing a witness in order to assess the advisability of bail or otherwise?'

'There's no *provision*, sir, but I have known such an occurrence. I have indeed. There is no provision specifically against it.'

'Thank you,' said Gunn, sitting back, and linking his fingers together. 'I would like to hear one of your witnesses, Miss Warrender, before making any decision. I trust,' he went on, peering down at Leeminster but more concerned with West's reaction, 'that the police have no objection.'

Leeminster, obviously taken off his guard, hesitated, then turned and sent a silent appeal across the courtroom to his superior. And on that instant, all eyes turned towards Chief Superintendent Roger West.

Chapter Two

DECISION

Roger West had been virtually sure what would happen, and there was no reason for him to hesitate; yet he did. Magistrates, even considerate ones like Gunn, had a certain sense of their position and did not like to have their decisions anticipated. Moreover, it was never wise to look slick and over clever in front of the Press; further, he did not want to make Leeminster feel small. So he paused for a few seconds before mouthing 'no objection' so that Leeminster could turn immediately and say, 'I've no objection, sir.'

'Then if Miss Warrender will call a witness, we can proceed.'

Soon, from the well of the court, came a buxom girl in her early twenties, fair-haired, blue-eyed, fresh-complexioned. She wore a loose-fitting, loose-knit jumper in sky blue and a black mini-skirt which showed very long, very white legs, tiny ankles and surprisingly small feet. She took the stand, hesitating about taking the oath on the Bible, until Rachel Warrender said,

'You *are* going to tell the truth, aren't you?'

'I certainly am.' The fair girl's lips had a tendency to pout, and were too-heavily lipsticked with bright red.

'That is all you're promising,' said Rachel.

'. . . so help me God,' said the girl.

'Your name,' demanded Farriman, formally.

'Maisie Dunster of 41, Concert Street, Chelsea, S.W.3,' stated the girl.

Farriman wrote very slowly, very deliberately, and the court paused as if for breath.

'Very well—please proceed.'

'Miss Dunster,' said Rachel Warrender, 'did you see the accused, Mario Rapelli, at all last evening?'

The witness's eyes were turned towards Rapelli, and she nodded.

'I did.'

'Will you tell the court what time you were with him?'

'From seven o'clock until nine,' answered the witness, precisely.

'Seven o'clock until nine,' echoed Charles Gunn, frowning. He had a feeling that this over-made-up young woman was enjoying herself, finding this appearance before the court quite fun. He felt disapproving, not at all sure that she would hesitate to perjure herself, but that wasn't his chief anxiety. It would be difficult to make sure that the evidence was keyed to the remand, and he had a feeling that Rachel Warrender proposed to bring evidence about the accusation. He alone was the authority in the court, and he alone could decide how far to let her go with her witnesses.

The fair girl, at all events, was under oath. He glanced down at Farriman, who came into his own at last.

'Will you please read the charge, Mr. Farriman, and all relevant statements made in court?'

'Gladly, sir! The police witness, on oath, stated that he called on the accused, Mario Lucullus Rapelli, at his home at eleven sixteen o'clock last night, Thursday, May 21st, and first cautioned and then charged him with assaulting a Mr. Ricardo Verdi at 17, Doons Way, Hampstead, last evening between eight o'clock and nine o'clock and of causing Mr. Verdi grievous bodily harm by striking him over the head with an electric guitar. The accused denied the charge. After cautioning the accused for a second time the witness stated he told him he was under arrest. He took him to the Mid-Western Divisional Police Station and there he was lodged for the night.'

Leeminster gave a little nod.

'Thank you,' Gunn said, and at last looked at the witness. Before he could speak, she burst out, 'He couldn't have attacked Ricky, he was with me, in Chelsea, *in my* flat.' Then she drew herself up and thrust her provocatively lifted bosom forward, adding in a ringing tone, 'In my bed! *And* I've two witnesses to prove it.'

Someone gasped; two or three tittered; the newspapermen made notes with great eagerness, and Maisie Dunster surveyed the court with an air of triumph at having created a sensation. And she had. Gunn kept his self-control with an effort. He should have questioned the witness himself, of course; by allowing Rachel Warrender to do so he had invited trouble. It was partly because he wanted to hear what would be said. Then, almost unbelieving, he saw Roger West stand up and ask in a most casual-seeming voice, 'As a point of interest, Miss Dunster, were the other two witnesses in your bed at the same time?'

Maisie Dunster turned to look at him.

'As a matter of fact, they *were*,' she said defiantly. 'Have you never heard of a sex-party?'

Charles Gunn sat very still and expressionless. He was of a generation which could still be shocked, yet not surprised, by Maisie Dunster's brazen statements; at such moments he concluded that he was much more Victorian than he had realised. But the essential thing was to rebuke West, and he said in his sternest voice, 'Superintendent, you have no right at all to intervene. Such intervention amounts to contempt of court, as you must know.'

Farriman, glaring at Roger, obviously agreed. West's expression was difficult to assess, and Gunn knew he had been fully aware of his offence but had taken the risk in order to throw some doubt on to the reliability of the witness.

'I am very sorry, sir,' he said. 'Very sorry.'

Gunn growled, 'Very well. I will overlook your intervention. As for the witness's evidence, I do not see its relevance to the issue of a remand.' He glowered at Rachel Warrender, then went on in a clipped voice, 'The accused is remanded for eight days on two sureties other than himself of five hundred pounds each. Will you make any arrangements you think necessary below the court,' he added to Rachel Warrender. 'Failing the two sureties then of course the accused must remain in custody.' He rapped the bench with his gavel. 'Next case, please.'

Almost at once, the two policemen by the dock helped Rapelli out. Perhaps the most remarkable thing was that the prisoner obviously needed physical support, being so very near collapse. Rachel Warrender hurried after him, while the newspapermen crowded round Maisie. Once she was outside the door of the courtroom, cameras began to click ...

*   *   *

There in the *Globe* was a front-page picture of Maisie Dunster and, in the background and coming out of the courtroom, was Roger West. Among the people who saw the picture and read the story was Commander Coppell, chief executive of the Criminal Investigation Department of New Scotland Yard, as he sat back in his car after a very late luncheon at the Guildhall. Coppell, a heavy, rather sultry-looking man with smooth, shiny black hair, sat up, read the story in detail, then glowered out of the window at the traffic in the Strand. It was nearly four o'clock before he reached his office. A rather prim and over-zealous secretary was at the door as he opened it.

'The assistant commissioner would like you to call him, sir.'

'Get him,' growled Coppell. He went to his desk and sat down, opened the *Globe* out before him and reread the article. Almost at once his telephone bell rang.

'The assistant commissioner,' announced his secretary.

Coppell grunted, and then said, 'You want me, sir?'

'What can you tell me about this Rapelli case?' enquired the assistant commissioner, who was the chief of the C.I.D. department and directly responsible to the commissioner.

'Only what I've read in the *Globe*,' growled Coppell.

'Didn't you know about it this morning?' The assistant commissioner sounded surprised.

'Oh, West told me about the arrest and said he wanted to ask for an eight-day remand. He didn't suggest there was anything out of the ordinary about it.' Coppell's voice was raw with an overtone of complaint. 'Or any doubt.'

'There appears to be a great deal of doubt,' remarked the assistant commissioner. He was an able man who was inclined to veer whichever way the wind was blowing, not one to stand much on his own. 'Do you know if West had been informed of the alibi story?'

'I've been out to the Guildhall, that Commonwealth Police Conference luncheon, and only just got back,' Coppell said defensively. 'I'll see West at once.'

'Let me know what he has to say,' ordered the assistant commissioner. 'The Home Office is extremely disturbed.'

'Soon as I can,' promised Coppell.

He put down the receiver and glowered out of a window which overlooked a mammoth new building and showed a silvery slip of the Thames. He picked up the receiver of a telephone which was connected with his secretary, and as she answered he demanded, 'Do you know if Superintendent West is in?'

'I have no idea, sir.'

'Then find out and let me know. Don't let him know I've enquired.' Coppell put down the receiver, stood up and changed the direction of his glower; he could now see Lambeth Bridge and a corner of the roof of the Houses of Parliament through a haze caused by a slight drizzle. He was a proud man, and particularly proud of his position; and he was very jealous of it. West had broken the first rule of a hearing; spoken to the court when not under oath. Even apart from that, he had been grossly inefficient: he should have made sure there was no alibi before authorising Rapelli's arrest.

Rapelli—Rapelli. The name rang a bell, but he could not call the bell to mind. Well, it didn't greatly matter, what mattered was that West be called on to explain his actions. He had certainly made trouble for himself by his intervention in court, and his crack about the other witnesses being in the same bed would have some nasty repercussions, despite his having apparently hit the nail on the head.

Coppell's secretary called.

'Mr. West has just gone into his office, sir.'

'Right,' said Coppell. 'If anyone wants me, that's where I'll be.'

*   *   *

'I always knew West would go too far one day,' Coppell's secretary said to the assistant commissioner's secretary, half an hour later. 'Wouldn't I like to know what's going on in West's office!'

'You'll be the first to hear,' the assistant commissioner's secretary replied, tartly. She had a very soft spot for Roger West but for some reason the other woman was always spiteful towards him. Could he have snubbed her at some time? The assistant commissioner's secretary had no way of telling, but she wished there were a way to warn West of the ill-will that Coppell's secretary had for him.

*   *   *

Roger West was in a mood halfway between anger and chagrin when he turned into his office, for this was a day when nothing would go right. He hadn't lunched and was both hungry and slightly headachy, which showed a little in the glassiness of his eyes. He had an office of his own but no secretary, drawing from the secretarial pool whenever he needed a stenographer, which wasn't often. A small office next door was a detective sergeant's—named Danizon—who acted as his general assistant, sheltered him from too much interference and did everything possible to make life easy for him.

Roger opened his door and Danizon jumped up from a small desk jammed into a corner.

'Sir?'

'Tea and sandwiches, please,' Roger said. 'I'm famished.'

'Right away, sir.'

'Anyone been after me?'

'No one in particular,' answered Danizon. 'The sureties failed to put up the money for Rapelli, so he's been taken to Brixton.'

'Can't say I mind,' Roger said, but he was puzzled. After making such a plea in court, why hadn't Rachel Warrender provided the sureties?

'Did you have any luck?' Danizon asked.

Roger shook his head and went back to his own room.

There were a few messages, mostly from the divisions, one
notice of a Police Union meeting, one advance notice of
the Metropolitan Police Ball, which would be early in
October. There was a pencilled note across the corner
of this. *'Care to be M.C.?'* In this mood I wouldn't like
to be Master of Ceremonies at a five shilling hop, Roger
thought, scowling; then he realised the absurdity of his
own mood, and grinned. He was still smiling broadly,
without knowing that it made him look quite startlingly
handsome and carefree, when the door from the passage
opened and Coppell strode in.

Roger had no time to change his expression, which
froze into a set grin as Coppell slammed the door behind
him.

'You've got a hell of a lot to be happy about,' he
growled. 'I expected you to be in tears.'

There wasn't any doubt about Coppell's mood; he was
out for blood. And there wasn't the slightest point in
answering back in the same tone. The best way to answer
Coppell was earnestly.

'What should I be crying about, sir?'

'As if you didn't know.'

Roger hesitated, rounded his desk, and pushed a chair
into position so that Coppell could sit down. But Coppell
preferred to grip the back of the wooden armchair, in
much the same way as Rapelli had gripped the rail of
the dock that morning. His heavy jowl looked fuller than
usual, his mouth was tightly set, his deepset eyes sparked
with irritation.

Roger stood behind his desk.

'I've drawn four blanks today,' he observed. 'But some
days are like that.'

'When you can spare a minute,' Coppell said with heavy
sarcasm, 'you might tell me what cases went sour on you,
and why. You can begin with Rapelli's arrest. From where

I stand, it was bad enough to send Leeminster to arrest
and charge him without being sure he was guilty, but
why in hell you persisted in the charge, and then committed contempt of court with that crack about him and
the witnesses I shall never understand.'

Roger said in a thin voice, 'Won't you, sir?'

'No. What the hell got into you?'

Very slowly and deliberately Roger pushed his swivel
chair into position behind his desk and sat down. He had
known what he was doing, and Coppell must realise that;
to adopt this attitude was to condemn him before he had
been heard. For a few moments he was too angry to speak,
but losing his temper would serve no purpose. He looked
straight into Coppell's eyes, and schooled his voice to
carry a tone of cool respect.

'I might understandably ask you the same question:
what has got into you?'

As he spoke, he knew that it had been the wrong
moment; that instead of pulling Coppell up sharply into
a more reasonable mood it had put him high on his
dignity. Out of the blue, as it were, another crisis was
upon him; you didn't force a quarrel with your superior
if you wanted to concentrate on the job in hand. And
Coppell had a lot of influence in high places, could
present him favourably if he wished and nearly damn
him if he chose to be malicious.

Just now, he looked as if he hated Roger, and he
actually took a long step forward, as if to sweep the
younger man aside.

Chapter Three

CONFLICT

Coppell paused.

That he was genuinely angry showed in the glitter in his eyes and the swarthy flush in his cheeks. Roger wondered what was going on in his mind. Was he thinking much as he, Roger, was thinking: that, angry and resentful though he felt, there was no point in pushing a quarrel? They were mature men, very senior officials, and they should have sufficient self-respect and respect for each other to avoid open conflict. His own anger began to fade but Coppell's apparently remained. Suddenly it dawned on him that Coppell was now in such a towering rage that he could hardly control himself.

So, he made himself say, 'I'm sorry, sir.'

Coppell glowered and growled, 'What's that?'

'I said I was sorry, sir.'

Coppell was only five years Roger's senior in age and service. Everyone who was anyone at the Yard knew that he had been appointed commander because there had been no one else of sufficient experience for the job. Only the discipline of the Yard, the absolute rule that on duty no officer called a senior in rank by his Christian name, and always used the 'sir' held Roger steady now, but his heart was thumping and some of his nerves began to quiver. He couldn't do more.

Oh, grow *up*, he thought: and he was thinking of

himself, not Coppell. He was suddenly aware that in one way Coppell would never grow up, would probably never know true magnanimity. But at least the 'sorry' mollified him and his eyes lost their glitter.

Would Coppell rub his nose in the apology?

If he says I should damn well think so, thought Roger in another surge of emotion, I'll give him my resignation.

Coppell opened his mouth to speak, but before he uttered a word the door of the communicating room with Danizon opened and Danizon himself came in, pushing the door open with his rump. A tray rattled in his hand. Coppell, nearer the door, acted almost mechanically, and held it for the detective sergeant to come through. Danizon must have known that someone was there but not who it was. He grunted 'ta' and placed the laden tray on a corner of Roger's desk. There was tea, hot water, milk, sandwiches thick with meat, bread and butter and some jam.

'Best I could do, sir,' said Danizon, then for the first time saw Roger's face. He broke off, his expression asking, 'What have I done wrong?' Then he glanced round and saw who had held the door open for him.

Out of the blue, Roger had a thought that was almost inspired, and he said, 'Fetch another cup for the commander, sergeant.'

'Er—yes sir!' Danizon could not get out of the room quickly enough, and he shot one agonised glance over his shoulder as the door closed on him.

Coppell gave a kind of grin.

'Training him for the canteen?' he asked.

'I missed lunch,' Roger replied, and wondered whether the incident would restore Coppell to a reasonable mood.

'Doing what?' asked Coppell, and then he snorted. 'Looking for those other two who were in bed with Rapelli?'

That appealed to him; if he, Roger, went carefully they would be over the worst, although the conflict between them would probably never fade entirely.

Before he could answer, Coppell snorted again.

'Well, let's hear more. You wouldn't stick your neck out unless you had a reason, even if a bloody bad reason. The Home Office is on the warpath, so your explanation had better be good.'

Roger's heart dropped.

'There's been a lot of cannabis and some heroin pushed in and around Doons Way, which is a short street with some small clubs and a lot of noise,' he stated. 'I thought that the man Rapelli was involved. I was afraid that if Rapelli was out on bail he himself might be attacked next.'

'You just thought,' breathed Coppell.

'I also knew that some of the clubs stage occasional sex orgies in the upper rooms and that this witness—Dunster—runs around with some pretty funny people. All-in-all, I decided it was worth letting the witness and her counsel and the court know what I knew. And I gambled on Gunn letting it pass with an apology.'

'Just as you gambled on quietening me down with one,' Coppell said.

Then Danizon came in with a cup and saucer, looking almost pleadingly at Roger for approbation. Roger took the cup and saucer.

'Thanks. Oh, sergeant—has Mid-Western Division called?'

'Not—not lately, sir.'

'If anyone calls from there, put the call through to me.'

'Right, sir!' Danizon backed out with obvious relief, and Roger began to pour tea. At least he knew that Coppell liked his strong, with plenty of sugar.

'We've so much drug pushing going on I think the

gamble was worth it. But I can't see Rachel Warrender defending anyone involved in drugs. I think the alibi was a phoney,' he went on, 'but I'm not sure drugs are the trouble. I *am* sure Rapelli's terrified.'

'There *are* orgies,' Coppell pointed out. 'The alibi could be genuine.'

'Yes, indeed.' Roger handed him a cup of tea and held out the sugar bowl. 'But if the Dunster girl is telling the truth, then two witnesses that *I* have, who swear they saw Rapelli's attack on Verdi, are lying. And I don't think they are.'

'Now I begin to see daylight,' breathed Coppell. 'You think the defence was trying to discredit police witnesses in advance?'

'I haven't the slightest reason to think our witnesses are lying,' Roger replied. 'I've seen them both after the court hearing. Had to go to a cabinet-making factory in Wandsworth for one and a bakery in Bethnal Green for the other, but their evidence will be all we need. I had to make sure of that, in view of what I'd done in court.'

Coppell gulped down his tea.

'So you've some sense. And we've two witnesses against Rapelli's three,' he went on, musingly.

'I can't imagine any jury believing the sex-party evidence,' said Roger. 'The Dunster girl is perfectly capable of that sort of thing, as I said, all the same—' He paused.

Coppell looked at him intently.

'Carry on.'

'Well, sir—' Roger paused again. 'The whole thing's too slick, too convenient for Rapelli, for my liking. The girl's a thorough bad lot all right, and more than capable of perjuring herself, which was what I meant to show the court when I said what I did. But even though I myself gave it to her on a plate—' Roger smiled ruefully '—I'm just not happy about this alibi.'

Coppell frowned.

'What do you intend doing now?' he asked.

'Well, sir, I'd like to check on who else was supposed to be participating in the fun and games at Maisie Dunster's apartment. I tried this afternoon, in fact, but no one was home. The apartment is in an old house converted into flats or flatlets, and all the tenants seem to work. They were out, anyway. Then I tried to get a line on Rachel Warrender's recent activities, but drew a blank. Her father is the Member of Parliament and the firm of Warrender, Clansel and Warrender is a very old and reputable one. None of the partners was in and none of the clerks would talk about the girl. I also tried to get a line on Rapelli's recent movements, and again drew a blank. He says he's a translator for magazines and publishers of English into Italian and vice versa, but nothing much has turned up about him. I can't yet prove he's involved in drugs.' Roger gave a short, rueful grimace. 'And when I started out this morning I thought we might really have a line on the drug business, while the case against Rapelli seemed cut and dried. It wasn't until Rachel Warrender came to see me and threatened to produce her witnesses for Rapelli that things began to misfire.'

Coppell's eyes rounded.

'She did *what*?'

'Only half an hour before Rapelli was due in the dock. I went over to the court as soon as I could and arrived just in time. I wanted to make sure Leeminster wasn't on his own when she arrived. If there was going to be trouble, I wanted to be in the middle of it.'

'You certainly are that,' growled Coppell. 'Where are the defence witnesses now?'

'Division is checking up on them,' answered Roger, and I expect word any time.' When Coppell didn't speak, he went on, 'It's a peculiar case in every way. Ricardo Verdi and some friends were at a small private club, where they have so-called musical evenings—a record club, I gather, with some instrument playing. Division now says there's no evidence of pot or of anything erotic —the members like off-beat music and go there to enjoy it. Something happened between Rapelli and Verdi and Rapelli struck Verdi over the head with an electric guitar.'

Coppell echoed, 'A guitar?'

'A heavy, ornamental one,' confirmed Roger. 'I went to see him this afternoon—he's at the Hampstead Cottage Hospital. The surgeon said that he—Verdi—has an exceptionally thin skull. There is some brain damage and some haemorrhage.'

'What are his chances?' demanded Coppell.

'No more than fifty-fifty,' Roger answered.

'So it might turn out to be a murder charge,' Coppell remarked. 'Handsome, if Rapelli did do this job, then we want absolute proof. Absolute, understand. And we won't have it until you break this alibi, and that means proving that three people are lying. And if they are lying —why? Give me one good reason.'

'To save Rapelli from being convicted,' Roger answered flatly. 'Well, if they are lying then I'll soon find out.'

Coppell frowned.

'You've got just seven days.'

'It ought to be enough.'

'If you can't produce positive evidence that the alibi is phoney by the second hearing, the case will probably be dismissed,' Coppell said, 'and that won't do you any good.'

Until that moment, Roger had been prepared to let the situation ease away, but suddenly anger flared up in him again. There was something very close to a threat, certainly a sneer, in Coppell's manner and words. He had swung back to his unreasonable, almost bullying manner, and if Roger let it pass then he would always be at Coppell's mercy. So he schooled himself to ask calmly, 'It wouldn't do me any great harm, surely?'

'Like hell it wouldn't!'

'I hate to remind you,' said Roger, icily now, 'that of the crimes brought to the Yard's notice in the past four years, over fifty per cent have remained unsolved. Yet barely twenty per cent of those I've personally investigated have been unsolved. Aren't I allowed a failure without being covertly threatened with disciplinary action?'

Coppell turned a dusky turkey-red.

'You're being bloody-minded,' he rasped. 'You may not have a high opinion of me or the Yard's performance while I've been commander, but let me tell you that a lot of people *do* have a high opinion of me. And you're the only senior officer around from whom we've had any bad publicity.' He clenched his fist and banged it on the folded copy of the *Globe*. 'And that's the worst kind of publicity.'

He turned on his heel, and strode out; the door slammed behind him.

Roger did not move for some minutes, just sat there like a statue, his face the colour of white marble. His features were set, his full lips drawn very tight, his eyes narrowed beneath the well-shaped brows.

He was not conscious of thought; barely, of feeling. He felt cold, and once or twice a quiver ran through his whole body. A phrase from childhood was the first thought that came into his mind: *as if someone were walking over my grave*. Slowly, he forced himself to relax, and getting up, he went to the window and looked out at the complex of modern buildings. It was overcast and there was a spit of rain in the air. He opened the window and although the air was cold and damp, he was glad of it. He needed fresh air.

It was several minutes before he went back to the desk, sat down and pulled the *Globe* towards him. On the front page was the story of a right-wing rally at the Albert Hall, addressed by George Entwhistle, the anti-immigrant M.P., and Sir Roland Warrender, but he did not read these, apart from the headlines. He turned to the article that had so upset Coppell, and read every word closely. A change came over him. This article was slanted—slanted against him and against the police—even to some degree, against the magistrate.

One phrase read:

> *Since when, in British courts, have the police been authorised to speak except under oath?*

Another ran:

> *Chief Superintendent West is one of the Yard's most experienced officers. He has a good reputation as a resourceful and often courageous man. What therefore induced him not only to commit such contempt of court but also to imply—as undoubtedly he did imply—that there was some kind of sex orgy taking place at the flat of the young woman who had just given evidence in defence of the accused? We do not like to believe that such a highly placed officer desired to discredit a witness, but the consequence of his remark: 'As a point of interest, Miss Dunster, were the other two witnesses in your bed at the same time?' . . .*

Roger read on, slowly.

There were no paragraphs which he could lift out as being, in fact, defamatory, but the whole tenor of the article was critical of the police in general as well as of his handling of this case in particular. At last, he put the paper aside. He had a pressure headache behind the eyes, and a heavy feeling of depression in his breast, like a physical weight. By chance, the paper closed to the front page, and he saw the Entwhistle and Warrender speeches. There was a lead-in by the *Globe* political correspondent.

> *Compared with Sir Roland, Mr. Entwhistle's speech was pure Liberalism, all honey and tolerance. Sir Roland, on the other hand, called again for a Business-man's Government—and government by decree. There is much in what he says ...*

The ringing of the telephone made Roger start; he let it ring again, picked it up and then announced 'West,' in a very quiet voice.

'Superintendent Cole of North Western is on the line, sir.'

'Ah. Thanks.' The call and the fact that it might bring some good news jolted Roger out of his depression, and he went on, 'Blackie?'

'Just one moment, sir,' a man responded.

Perhaps it was as well that he had a few moments in which to think. Blackie Cole had charge of a curiously mixed division. Some parts of Hampstead were exclusive and expensive, boasting many of the most opulent homes in London. Others were overcrowded; big, once proud homes had been divided into flats. There and all about the village were 'clubs' which were little more than excuses for smoking pot, for sex-parties, for perversion of all kinds. It was most discreetly done, partly because Cole had the district under very tight control. He knew practically everything that went on, when to jump on a 'club' which was moving from pot to heroin and other more

injurious drugs, when sex-parties were being overdone.
He was renowned for his skill in picking out clubs where
a number of new 'members' from the provinces were
starting the pot habit. He raided these and had a remarkable number of successes in sending teenagers back to
their homes and away from the temptations of London's
lower night life.

At last, Cole came on the line.

'Sorry to keep you, Handsome. I had a call which might
have changed my report but instead it's strengthened it.
I feel very bad that I didn't have this for you earlier. The
Doon Club is quite genuine and wholly free from drugs.
I've checked on twenty-one of its membership of thirty,
and there isn't a whisper of suspicion. There's not even
any reason to believe that they show obscene movies or
slides. All the evidence is that they go to listen to and
make music and discuss it afterwards.' Cole paused, only
to go on before Roger could speak. 'There doesn't appear
so far the slightest motive for Rapelli to attack Verdi, but
there is one piece of odd information. The two witnesses
of the attack—the men you saw—are new members. They
joined at the same time, one day last week. I would have
a go at them if I were you: they could be lying.'

Chapter Four

SHOCK

Roger put the telephone down slowly after Cole had rung off. It was pointless to jump to conclusions, but all the time Cole had been talking his depression, only briefly vanquished, came back and grew much heavier. Cole, a shrewd man who was cautious enough seldom to put a foot wrong, made it clear that he thought the police witnesses could have lied. And if only one of them could be discredited, then the police case would crash and the alibi witnesses could be triumphant.

Coppell had sensed much of this, of course; that was why he had been incensed by the piece in the *Globe*. There was nothing surprising in that. With hindsight, the question which had seemed so pertinent in court had been a piece of folly. West gave a funny little laugh. Even Blackie Cole had assumed that he had fallen down on the job; it had not even occurred to him to ask if Roger had seen the two witnesses and checked their story.

Well, he'd seen them both, and it was time he put a report about them on paper.

Wilfred Smithson was a cabinet maker in a small factory near the River Wandle at Wandsworth, a big railway arch, painted green. Roger could picture him, white-aproned, standing at a wooden bench, shavings piled on the bench and about his feet, tools in their racks fitted to the wall. At the far end was a circular saw. All about

the arch was stacked timber, some already cut to size.
Smithson's job was very skilled: he made first-quality
furniture to customer's requirements. He earned about
thirty pounds in a five-day week, was single, and loved
music.

This last was indisputable, for radio music filled the
archway, sometimes so loud that it drowned the noise of
the band and circular saw, while Smithson had a small
tape-recorder on the bench and tiny earphones; he
listened to music of his own liking and contrived somehow to blot out the popular tunes from the radio.

Roger could also see him as a small, thin-faced, very
lean youth of perhaps twenty-one.

'I've never been so surprised in my life. They flew into
a temper, swearing at each other in Italian, I think, and
Rapelli grabbed Verdi's guitar and crowned him. Verdi
went out like a light.'

Smithson had seemed so transparently honest.

So had Hamish Campbell.

Campbell was a pastry-cook at a large bakery at Bethnal
Green, in the East End and right across London from
Smithson. He had been in a kitchen leading off the main
kitchen, with huge pans of dough, great electric ovens,
and everywhere the rich, all-pervading smell of baking
and new-baked bread. Campbell had been rolling pastry;
another, older man had been operating a machine for
cutting the pastry into shapes for tarts; these went on a
conveyor and the tarts were carried away and filled by a
feed nozzle. Roger could remember, fascinated, how the
nozzles disposed different kinds of filling from straw-
berry jam to lemon curd.

Campbell, plumpish, fair-haired, fresh-faced and
freckled, had honest-looking brown eyes.

'Rapelli just snatched the guitar away and biffed Verdi
over the head with it—almost as if the music was driving

him mad. Blimey! I can hear the bang now—broke the instrument *and* Verdi's head.'

'Did Rapelli say anything?' Roger had asked.

'No,' Campbell had answered. 'He turned and walked away. I could see Verdi's head was bleeding something cruel, so I phoned the police and said they needed an ambulance. Wilf—that's my mate—he gave Verdi some first aid. He's a carpenter, see, used to people cutting themselves with chisels and saws. He's got his first-aid certificate. If you ever cut yourself he's your man.'

The divisional report corroborated the story; division had found Smithson giving capable first aid by padding the wound and stopping the bleeding. He and Campbell had both made statements to the police, and Leeminster, who had been the divisional officer in charge that night, had had no reason to doubt their story.

Roger finished the handwritten report, and felt less anxious and troubled. He rang for Danizon, who came in promptly, looking freshly washed and brushed.

'Have these typed—the usual report copies,' Roger ordered, and added, 'no—make it two more than the usual number.'

'Will—er—will the morning do?' asked Danizon.

'Why not this afternoon?' asked Roger, and glanced at his watch. 'Good Lord—it's six-fifteen! Yes, the morning will do. I'll keep these meanwhile. You get off.' He forebore to ask where the sergeant was so anxious to go, put the reports in his brief-case to read at home, and then sat back and reflected over the day. He still could not think of Coppell without a rising sense of indignation, and that in itself was enough to make him disgruntled. He pushed his chair back and was about to get up when his telephone bell rang.

'Superintendent West,' he almost barked.

There was a slight pause before a familiar voice sounded.

'Hi, Dad!'

'Scoop!' Roger exclaimed, and could picture the big face of his elder son, Martin-called-Scoop; and also could imagine the faint smile on it.

'Don't sound so horrified,' Scoop said, in a rather troubled voice.

'Just surprised!' said Roger. 'It must be a year since you called me at the office. I—is everything all right?' he diverged suddenly. For on the last occasion Martin had telephoned him at the Yard it was to tell him that Janet, his wife, had fallen down some stairs and was at the hospital awaiting a doctor's report.

'Er—no one's fallen down and broken their neck,' Scoop said in his slightly rueful, half-jesting way. 'But— I—er—I'd like a talk with you, Pop. Er—Dad. Er—I mean, not with the family. It—er—well, Mummy's been a bit—er—well, impatient lately and I—er—'

'We can have a drink, or a meal, or you can come here,' Roger said quietly. 'I can telephone your mother and say I'll be late.'

'Well, no need for that, anyhow,' said Scoop. 'She's gone to the pictures with Richard and Lindy, and won't be back until elevenish. So home would do fine tonight.'

'I'll be there in half an hour,' promised Roger.

He was outside and in his car within five minutes, and within twenty was at one end of Bell Street, Chelsea, the street where he and Janet had lived since their marriage, nearly thirty years ago. At one end was the wide thoroughfare of King's Road, at the other another street which led to the Chelsea Embankment. There was a drizzle over the Thames and everywhere; the flowers and grass in the front gardens looked as if they were covered with dew; roofs and windows, fences and railings were all smeared with moisture; it was a most depressing day for May.

Roger parked out of sight of his house; he did not want to be early. If he knew Martin, the boy would be preparing a simple meal, and would like to have everything ready. He was not yet anxious, for Martin sometimes made mountains out of molehills, but he was eager to know what this S.O.S. was about. If it were something that could not be discussed about in the family, it might indeed be a cause for anxiety, for Janet got on remarkably well with her two sons.

One thing had been obvious from the moment he had heard that Janet was out with Richard and his girl-friend. Richard had deliberately taken his mother off to allow Scoop to have this 'personal talk'.

Roger moved away, and pulled into the garage at the side and slightly to the front of the house in Bell Street. It was a stucco-fronted building, almost square, with bow windows. Creepers and ramblers grew on the walls, the privet hedge was neatly trimmed, and so was the small front lawn. Late wallflowers and tulips looked bedraggled and forlorn in the borders.

Roger went in by the back door, to find Martin at the kitchen sink. He turned round and gave Roger a slow smile. His face was broad, like his forehead, and but for a broken nose—from an injury caused by boxing at school —he would have been remarkably handsome, although more like his mother than Roger. But he had Roger's full, generous-looking lips.

'Hi, Dad!'

'Hi, Scoop. What are you cooking?'

'Steak and sausages and chips. Okay?'

'Sounds wonderful. I had no lunch.' Roger went and contemplated the steaks and sausages under the grill, and saw the pan of oil already simmering, and the pile of chipped potatoes ready to be cooked. 'Ten minutes?'

'Fine.'

Roger went upstairs, washed, actually had time to sit back in the bedroom armchair for a few minutes before rejoining his son. The steaks and sausages were served and keeping warm under the grill; Scoop lifted a basket-scoop of golden-brown chips and put them in a deep, white, porcelain dish.

'Ever seen better French fries?' he boasted.

'Never. But what's the matter with plain English?'

'It's very out, to call chips chips,' Martin declared. 'Sit down, Pop.'

Roger sat at the big kitchen table, covered with a deceptively linen-like plastic tablecloth, and Martin placed a huge plate of food in front of him, then sat down opposite with as heaped a plate for himself.

Suddenly, he pushed plate and knife and fork away.

'Dad, I want to emigrate. Leave England, that is. For keeps. That is for keeps as far as I know. I've felt like it for a long time. Hate to seem ungrateful for all you and Mum have done for me, but—' He broke off, and gulped. 'Sorry, Dad.'

Roger was cutting through steak as Martin spoke, and he speared a piece on to his fork and raised it to his lips.

'You won't emigrate anywhere if you starve to death,' he remarked.

'Eh? Oh.' Martin gave an almost sheepish grin. 'I—er —I suppose you're right.' He pulled his plate back again. 'Aren't you shocked?'

'I'm mildly surprised,' Roger declared. 'But shocked—no. Why should I be?'

'I—er—I thought you'd hate the idea.'

'It didn't occur to you that I might be glad to see the back of you?' There was a teasing gleam in his eyes and a teasing tone in his voice, but suddenly it occurred to him that this was no time to tease, that for a moment at

least, Martin was taking that remark seriously. Quite
suddenly the years rolled away and Roger was jesting
with the 'child' and immediately reassuring him; 'teasing'
had been a feature of their early family life and still was;
he had forgotten that Martin could be led on almost as
easily as Richard.

'No,' Scoop said. 'It hadn't.'

'That's good,' said Roger. 'I didn't quite mean what I
said.'

Martin smiled with surprisingly evident relief.

'*That's* good too!'

'Where do you plan to go?' inquired Roger, choosing
'plan' deliberately, thinking it would help to reassure
Scoop that there would be no opposition to overcome
with him. But it was already evident why he had wanted
this talk alone, for Janet would hate the idea of emigration.

'Australia,' Scoop answered promptly.

'I suppose that's as good as any and no doubt better
than most,' remarked Roger.

He ate in silence for a few moments, and so did Martin,
whose hunger was getting the better of him. He, Roger,
was in fact feeling a delayed shock effect. He had known
for years that Martin wasn't too happy in England, that
life hadn't gone too well for him, but he had seen this in
terms of getting a better job, or having a breakthrough
with his painting. Scoop spent every moment of his spare
time with brush and easel.

'Really not shocked?' Martin asked after a while.

'No, Scoop. Not shocked, but I think Mummy will be.'

'Didn't I know it!' Scoop could hardly have sounded
more rueful.

'How long has it been since you made up your mind?'

'Oh, about a month,' Scoop told him, then coloured
and went on with a rush, 'I wanted to be absolutely sure

before I said anything, so I've been along to Australia House, and seen the New South Wales people and made an application for an assisted passage—it only costs ten pounds. Did you know?'

'Yes,' said Roger, and added rather heavily, 'so you've gone as far as that?'

Scoop nodded, without saying a word.

'Decided what ship yet?' asked Roger.

'The *Northern Star*,' answered Scoop. 'It's due to sail on June 28th.' He picked up his fork only to put it down again, almost awkwardly. 'Dad, I—I had to go ahead. I knew if I talked to you you'd have to tell Mummy, you wouldn't keep that kind of secret from her, and if Mummy had known she would have worked on you—well, on me too—to dissuade me. And—and well, I thought if everything was cut and dried then there couldn't be so much argument—er—discussion, I mean, and perhaps it wouldn't hurt so much.'

Roger looked at him steadily; and looking, he saw the tears close to the boy's eyes, a boy of twenty-one, a young man, so fearful of hurting that he had felt constrained to keep this tremendous yearning to himself. He felt a great warmth of feeling towards and a compelling need to reassure him and yet he did not quite know what to say.

He was still undecided when the telephone rang. Martin's brow furrowed and he muttered, 'Oh, damn!'

Chapter Five

OFFER

The last thing Roger wanted at that moment was a summons to the Yard, and Martin's muttered imprecation told him how his son felt. He pushed his chair back, and for some reason was more aware of the shock of the boy's news than he had been earlier. Before he was on his feet, Martin was up and halfway to the extension just in the passage by the kitchen door.

'I'll get it,' he said.

Roger watched and listened. The boy's voice was deep and pleasing, his manner nearly always the same: gentle and kindly. He was broad-shouldered and very powerful but the gentleness always hovered in his experience, in his grey eyes, in the way he handled animals and tools.

Now he said, 'This is Martin West ... Yes, I think so ... Who wants him, please? ... If you'll just hold on, I'll see ... Are you from Scotland Yard? ... Oh, thank you....' He appeared in the doorway, obviously surprised, looking ten years younger than his twenty-one. 'It's a Mr. Benjamin Artemeus,' he reported, 'and he would like to have a word with you. He's not from the Yard.'

'Then I'd better speak to him,' Roger said, and as he passed Martin he added quietly, 'I won't go out until we're through.' He reached the telephone and announced, 'Roger West speaking.'

'Mr. West,' began a man in a very pleasing voice, continuing without preamble, 'I would very much like to meet you and discuss a proposition which I think will interest you.'

It was a suspicious kind of opening and Roger became very wary indeed. He even ran through his mind the cases he was handling or involved in at the Yard; attempts to bribe often began in this way.

'What kind of proposition?' he enquired.

'It is wholly legal,' Artemeus declared, with an un-mistakable hint of laughter in his voice. 'Are you free for lunch tomorrow? I hope you are. I can make an offer which may be of great interest to you. And do let me repeat that it is wholly legal and for the time being, strictly confidential.'

'I'm not free for lunch on any such flimsy basis,' Roger said bluntly. 'What is this all about?'

There was a long pause, before the other man answered in an equally direct way, 'A position for you whenever you retire from the Metropolitan Police, Mr. West. I cannot discuss it over the telephone but it would be most advantageous to you. I feel sure you would be ill-advised not to discuss it.'

'What gives you the idea that I might retire?' asked Roger sharply.

'Oh, come. You're bound to retire sooner or later. The offer I can make may persuade you to do so early rather than late, but there will be no attempt to bring any pressure to bear on you. I—ah—would know better than to attempt such a manoeuvre with such a man.'

Roger was turning the whole thing over in his mind, very quickly.

He was free tomorrow, as far as he knew, and one day he *would* begin to think about retirement. Not yet, but one day, and many more conflicts with Coppell *might* make it sooner. Every senior policeman began to think, after a while, about his future; a pension would give a sufficiency but no luxury.

'I am free tomorrow, at the moment,' he said at last. 'But an urgent job might crop up and prevent me from keeping an appointment.'

'That is quite understood,' said Artemeus. 'Tomorrow at twelve-thirty, shall we say. At the Savoy Grill? ... Excellent ... I shall know you on sight, Mr. West, so I needn't give you any description of me. Good-night.'

He rang off, almost as if he wanted to avoid giving Roger time to change his mind. Roger rang off more slowly, repeating to himself several times, 'Twelve-thirty, Savoy Grill.' He sauntered back to the kitchen. Martin, finishing the chips, got up and took a big deep-dish apple-pie from the oven and placed it in front of Roger.

'Cream coming up ... Mum made this, it's gorgeous. Coffee?'

'Yes, please.'

Martin made instant coffee with water so hot that the powder fizzed and bubbled. Then he sat down again and grinned as broadly.

'Someone trying to bribe you, Pop?'

'Let them try,' said Roger, offhandedly. 'Now, where were we?' He poured thick cream over the pie, and out of the blue was reminded of Hamish Campbell. Pushing the thought aside, he went on, 'So you're really set on going to Australia?'

'I—I'm afraid I am,' Martin confirmed, with apologetic stubbornness.

'Can you tell me why?'

The boy hesitated, as he so often did, then answered very quietly, 'I haven't made much of a fist here at home, Dad. I don't blame conditions or—or taxes, or the way the country's run, I just—well, I just don't seem to fit in. There are a hundred reasons, really, but most of all I—

er—well I—er—I would like to make a fresh start in a new country with new ideas. I just'—he was speaking with great deliberation and yet almost stammered—'I just can't sit around here in England, with nothing really to look forward to, and—let's face it, Dad—not much hope of getting anywhere with my painting. I love England but it *is* tradition-bound, isn't it?'

'Are you sure Australia won't be?' asked Roger.

'Obviously I can't be sure but I don't think it will be in the same way,' Martin said. 'And it *is* British. I mean, it's in the Commonwealth, it's not like going to an entirely foreign country, is it?'

'You mean, it doesn't make you feel you're deserting England?' Roger put his spoon down and looked very straightly into his son's eyes. Martin seemed more than a little uncomfortable.

'I suppose that's what I do mean,' he admitted at last. Then with a burst of honesty which was characteristic of him, he went on, 'It's the only thing that's held me back, Dad. That you'd feel I was deserting Britain.' Then he went on with a kind of reluctant stubbornness, 'I don't honestly think I can do much to help England, but I'd hate to feel I was letting you down—or I'd hate to feel *you* thought so.'

Obviously he was crying out for reassurance: but knowing him, Roger was sure that he would not want any comment which sounded remotely glib. In any case, Roger wanted to learn more of what was in his mind.

'What about your mother?' he asked quietly.

'She's different,' Martin replied.

'How different?'

'I know it's bound to hurt her,' replied Martin, 'but no more than it would hurt any mother when her son finally leaves home. In a funny way it might hurt her less than if I were to get married. She—' He broke off, floundering, then went on almost grimly: 'Her reaction will be personal and emotional. Yours—well, yours will be emotional too, of course, but not in the same way. You're such a passionate Englishman, Dad.'

'I am!' gasped Roger.

'Gosh, yes! English standards of behaviour, English democracy, integrity, honesty—you believe in all these things so much. You're always saying that we have to stand and fight back, that we've lost so many of these standards but ought to try to regain them. Surely you know that?'

Roger drew in a deep breath.

He did know it, of course; he knew how bitterly disappointed he often was with the state of England, the standard of behaviour, the way the numbers of crimes committed had shot up, more than doubling themselves since he had joined the Force. But he hadn't realised that he had talked forcefully of these things so often that they had registered so much on his son. Watching the boy, whose face was set in unmistakable determination, he reminded himself sharply that this was Martin's problem, not his; that he had only one consideration: to help, reassure and even strengthen the lad's certainty.

So he smiled, and with a rare gesture leaned across the table and pressed his son's hand.

'Things were very much the same between the two wars,' he remarked. 'Before I met your mother and joined the police I was very tempted to go overseas. I think I would have chosen Canada or the United States.' He pressed Martin's hand again, and went on, 'In every generation there are those who are driven by some inner compulsion to emigrate. It's a form of pioneering, and it's very deep in the British, in fact in most Europeans. I would say there is only one thing that should stop you.'

Martin stiffened.

'What's that?'

'If *you* feel you are running away or deserting your country. If you yourself felt like that you would probably always have it on your mind and it would reduce your chances of settling down, being contented, and doing well. Do you ever feel even remotely like that?'

Martin's gaze was very steady, and he took his time replying. At last he answered.

'No, father, I don't. I don't think I've anything to offer here. I really don't. If I think anything I feel—oh, gosh, it sounds so corny, but I feel a responsibility to *people*, not to places, not even to my own people. Just people. And, I can fulfil that wherever I am.'

'There's no doubt about that,' agreed Roger. 'Answer me one question.'

'Yes, of course.'

'Has anything driven you away from home? From your mother and me?'

'Good God, *no*!' Martin was aghast. 'Absolutely *no*.' He hesitated for a while before going on in a different tone, 'I feel in a way I've failed you. I simply can't stay here and sponge on you. I just have to make my own way independently. It's something in *me*, nothing to do with you or mother or Fish. I just *have* to go.'

Roger pushed his chair back, rounded the table, and put his arm about his son's shoulder. He felt the strength of muscle, the solidity, very much like his own. He stood like that, searching for the exact words to convey his feelings; it had never been so important that he should say exactly the right thing.

At last, he said, 'When you're gone, Scoop, I shall miss you; miss you terribly. But I shall envy you, too, and admire you because you had the courage I lacked when I was your age.'

He stopped.

He wondered: was that the right note? Was it right?

He felt his son's shoulders shaking a little; heard a convulsive sigh; a gulp, as for breath. Then he realised that Martin was crying. Not much, he would never cry much, but—crying. Tears actually fell. Roger withdrew his arm and then went to the sink and put more water in the kettle. His back to his son, he asked, 'Worried about your mother's reaction?'

There was a sniff. 'I—yes. Yes, I am.'

'You needn't be.'

After a pause Martin said in an almost incredulous voice, 'What?'

'You needn't be. Oh, she'll be hurt, you're quite right about that. But she won't fight it and she won't think you've let her down in any way. She won't reproach you. And in a way she'll be glad. As parents we can't be happy at the fact that you haven't found the right niche in England, can't be happy that you're obviously torn up inside.'

Martin was getting up and turning round, cheeks tear-stained, eyes opened wide in disbelief mingled with hope.

'Are you—are you sure?'

'We'll find out when she comes home,' Roger said. 'She won't be long. If you prefer me to tell her I will.'

'No,' said Martin in a strangled voice. 'I'll tell her.'

* * *

Roger had never been more proud of his wife, or more pleased, or more affectionate towards her, than as he watched while Scoop told her very simply what he wanted: what he meant to do. They were still in the kitchen, and the kettle was on for tea, while he, Roger, put biscuits and cheese and fruit cake out for Janet and for Richard when he came in from seeing Lindy to her house, near by. Janet, tall and attractive, with her dark hair touched with grey, a fresh complexion and green-grey eyes, sat in an old saddle-back chair while Martin perched on a corner of the kitchen table.

And then he finished, saying, 'I just have to go. I hate hurting you but I just have to go.'

Janet leaned forward, both hands outstretched in re-assurance.

'Of course you have to,' she said. 'I've known for a long time that you've been restless and unhappy. And—' she drew him towards her '—and as for hurting, darling, I'd be much more hurt if you stayed home and were miserable because you didn't think I could take it.'

'Oh, Mum!' Martin cried. 'Oh, Mum!'

Suddenly, he was on her lap, his head buried on her shoulder. Roger saw her glistening tears as she soothed him. The next moment there was the sound of a key turning in the front door, and a few seconds later Richard came along the passage, whistling until he breezed into the kitchen. Catching sight of Scoop and his mother, he exclaimed *sotto voce*, 'Gosh!'

Then he looked across at his father. He was tall and dark, well-dressed in an up-to-the-minute Carnaby Street style, and looking exactly what he was: a highly success-ful young man in his chosen occupation. He was in fact one of the most promising younger men in television pro-duction and directing. A year younger than Martin, he now looked about thirteen as he shot an almost agonised questioning look at Roger.

Roger cocked a thumb.

'Come and make the tea, Fish, will you?' he said. 'I want to nip along to the bathroom.'

Scoop was leaning against the sink, drinking tea, when Roger went back to the kitchen. Janet had tea and a piece of cake on a small table by her side. Richard was tucking into the biscuits and cheese, and saying, 'Anyone

else want apple-pie and cream before I woof up the lot?'
No one did.

*   *   *

Later, Roger sat downstairs, reading through his
reports, altering a word or two here, making changes of
emphasis, seeing all the people concerned, in his mind's
eye, and yet for once putting most of his attention on his
family. No matter what he said or even pretended to
himself, the fact of Scoop's going hurt. And if it hurt
him, what would Janet feel? He waited until he heard
doors close upstairs; she had been in to each boy to say
goodnight, an old children's days habit which asserted
itself at all times of emotional crisis. He heard her clear
'Goodnight, Scoop,' and then went upstairs. She was
already half-undressed, very pale, and her eyes were shiny
with tears.

'Hallo, darling,' he said. 'You were wonderful!'

That was the moment when she burst out crying ...

It was a long time before she stopped and got ready
for bed, but it was not long, once she was in bed, before
Roger heard her even breathing, and knew she was
asleep.

He felt very tired but lay awake for over an hour. As
the minutes passed, Scoop's face faded from his mind and
he could picture Rachel Warrender's and Mario Rapelli's.
He wondered whether they were sleeping, and whether
the divisional police were keeping Rapelli under proper
surveillance.

He thought of Maisie Dunster with her bright hair and
cherry-red lips; of Hamish Campbell and his chef's hat
and white smock; of Wilfred Smithson and his tape-
recorder and earphones. The odd thing was that he did
not give a thought to Coppell, nor even to Benjamin
Artemeus and the proposals he had promised to make.

Chapter Six

DEATH

The telephone woke Roger next morning, and he groped for it, aware of the daylight, of Janet next to him, of the harshness of the bedside bell. He lifted the receiver, nearly dropped it and so made more noise, muttered 'Blast it,' and then grunted, 'West here.'

'This is Blackie Cole,' a man said. 'Blackie. Are you awake, Handsome?'

Blackie! Swift pictures of Rapelli, Verdi, and everyone involved, flashed through Roger's mind.

'Yes. What's up?'

'Verdi's dead,' announced Blackie, and stopped after the brusque statement.

In a way it was a good thing he did, for Roger needed a few moments to recover. Verdi, dead of a blow with a guitar, making murder the charge against Rapelli, with two witnesses prepared to swear he had swung that bizarre weapon. Roger struggled to a sitting position and felt a pillow being pushed into the gap between the head panel and the small of his back. Bless Janet!

'And what?' he asked Cole.

'The witness, Wilfred Smithson, died in a road accident late last night,' stated Blackie flatly. 'Not a hit and run, but the driver was probably drunk.' He paused again and then added almost superfluously. 'That makes the pastry-cook even more important.'

Now there seemed not the slightest doubt that there was deep significance behind the Verdi affair. There had been yesterday's stubborn attempt to get dismissal of the charge and now this tragedy; together they were too much for a coincidence.

Roger said roughly, 'We must watch Campbell like lynxes.'

'I've got his home covered, back and front,' Blackie assured him. 'I thought you should know straight away.'

'You couldn't be more right,' Roger approved. The bedside clock told him that it was a little after six. Janet had snuggled down again and he thought she was more asleep than awake. 'Anything else?'

'No,' said Blackie, and gave a grim laugh. 'Isn't that enough?'

'What about the driver of the car?'

'He's a man named Fogarty, and we're holding him at North Kensington. The accident happened in Fulham at Fulham Broadway, just after eleven o'clock last night. The night man at North Ken tied Smithson in with your court affair and put word through at once. So we did a very quick job on Fogarty. Howard has all the details.'

'Thanks,' said Roger. At least that was one good thing.

He rang off, and got out of bed. Janet stirred but did not speak, perhaps her way of saying that she wanted to try to get off to sleep again. In a way he would be glad to be out of the house before she was up and there was more discussion about and with Scoop. There could be no argument: he had to start on this new stage of the investigation very quickly. After last night Janet should be all right; in a way it might even be better for her to have an hour with the boys on their own. He bathed, dressed, shaved, and was downstairs in twenty minutes, making tea and toast; he disliked starting out without anything to eat.

Half an hour after receiving the telephone call he was
driving through nearly deserted streets towards North
Kensington, only twenty minutes away. He passed two
dust-carts, some red Post Office vans, some milk-carts and
several newspaper boys on bicycles, before he pulled up
outside the Victorian red-brick building. A constable
standing outside the entrance regarded him at first with
disapproval and then, on recognition, almost with alarm.
Roger nodded and strode up the steps. The duty sergeant
in the charge room on the right of the main hall, was
yawning over some reports. He looked up, saw Roger, and
sprang to attention.

'Mr. West!'

'Who's in charge?' asked Roger.

'Superintendent Howard, sir. First on the right at the
top of the stairs,' he added as Roger began to turn away.

Roger went up the stairs two at a time, yet Howard,
a bulky man and near the end of his police service, was at
the open door of the room by the time Roger appeared.
He was swift-moving and fast-thinking, and as he shook
hands he said, 'You're after that driver we're holding,
aren't you?'

'Yes,' Roger said. 'Has he talked about it?'

'He mumbles to himself when he says anything at all,
says he didn't see the man on the zebra crossing, and
pretends to be half-drunk still. But we had a medical
report, Handsome.' Howard paused, obviously for effect,
and Roger obligingly asked, 'What's the report?'

'He didn't have enough alcohol in his blood to make
a kitten drunk,' stated Howard. 'He's stone cold sober,
just acting a hangover.'

'Oh,' said Roger, 'is he. Know anything about him?'

'We've got this,' said Howard, and led the way into the
room. On a small table on one side, away from Howard's
roll-top desk, was a collection of oddments obviously

taken from a man's pockets. There was also a Record
Card, with fingerprints and a general description. The
man's name was Patrick Fogarty, he was five feet ten
inches, blue-eyed, fair-haired, age thirty-seven ... there
were a number of distinguishing marks. He lived by
himself in a bed-sittingroom at a house in New King's
Road, Fulham, and he was employed by a large firm of
caterers as a van driver. He had a small car of his own,
a Morris 1000, which he had been driving at the time of
the accident.

'Have you had his room searched?'

'Damn it,' protested Howard, 'it's only a case of
drunken driving, even if the man he ran down was one
of your witnesses.'

'How did you know that?' asked Roger.

'Blackie mentioned it when he was on the telephone,'
Howard replied. 'Want to see Fogarty?'

'I'd better,' Roger said.

But the man was stretched out on the bed in his cell,
snoring away, as apparently he had been for some time.
The policeman on cell duty said he hadn't stopped snoring, once he had started. The description was accurate
enough except that it hadn't told how broad and thick
Fogarty was, as powerful-looking a man as Roger had
seen in a long time.

He went back upstairs. On a side table in Howard's
office were some oddments from Fogarty's pockets, including some keys. Thoughtfully, Roger looked at the
keys, and then said, 'I'd like to take these, and you'll need
a receipt.'

Howard hesitated, then handed Roger a slip of paper.
Roger signed, 'Keys taken from the man Fogarty now in
my possession,' thanked Howard, and drove to the Yard.

There, *Information* had particulars of Fogarty and
was briefed to get more about his background, employ-

ment and friends. Roger went up to his own office and checked with the switchboard about the Justice of the Peace on duty. A justice or a magistrate had to sign every search warrant, and Roger needed a warrant for Fogarty's place. As he went to see the Justices of the Peace on call, he reflected grimly that until yesterday's encounter with Coppell he would have searched the room and worried about the warrant afterwards.

The Justice of the Peace, who lived near by, was an even-tempered man who showed no resentment at being disturbed so early in the morning, and signed the warrant on Roger's brief statement of need.

Now, Roger was at the crossroads again. He should, he knew, take a second man with him to make the search, yet some impulse urged him to go alone. He had acted on impulse once already and still wasn't sure of the consequences. It was surely folly to take another risk. Nevertheless, perhaps because of a need to justify and prove himself, perhaps because he was still resentful at Coppell, and wanted to hand him the case on a plate, he decided to take a quick look on his own. If necessary he could return with another officer later.

It was a little after half past seven when he walked up the steps of the house in New King's Road, only a mile from his own home. This house was in a small terrace, quite well-kept, with seven names and seven bell-pushes on the side of the porch.

Fogarty lived on the third floor.

Reaching his room, Roger put one of the keys in the lock and turned it; it was the right one. He opened the door cautiously. The caution was instinctive, he had no reason to suspect that anyone else was in the room. It was dark, as if the curtains were drawn. Light from the passage shone on a bookcase with some heavy-looking, leatherbound books, and on a chair over which some women's clothes were draped. A bra, stockings, a girdle.

Good God! thought Roger, what was the matter with him? Why had he taken it for granted that there would be no one else here? If he were caught entering a woman's room by himself he really would be in trouble. Why hadn't he brought a man with him? He stood still for a moment until he could make out the breathing of whoever was sleeping there, and while waiting he became aware of stale perfume or powder.

He drew back, pulling the door to but not quite closing it for fear of waking whoever was inside; he had no choice at all, had to send for a man before searching; probably should not search at all.

Sensing rather than hearing movement, he half-turned, caught sight of the dark, shiny hair of a man bent low behind him. Then he felt hands thump against his shoulders and went hurtling forward, banging his forehead against the door. It swung open, and he fell headlong into the room. His head smacked against the floor, nearly stunning him, but he was aware of hands gripping his wrists and lifting his legs up, then pushing him to one side. The next moment he was kicked savagely in the ribs, then the door slammed and the light was shut out. He was here, alone, in darkness, gasping for breath.

Gasping.

He was aware of many things: mostly, fears.

What in heaven's name *had* made him come alone? He could imagine the ridicule if this story reached the newspapers! It would not only be personally damaging, it would seriously affect the Yard. *Coppell*. How could he have taken such a chance? A rookie would have known better!

He heard a sound; of creaking.

He was not breathing so heavily now, and when he concentrated he was aware of someone else breathing.

The woman of course; the woman whose clothes were on the chair.

Was she getting out of bed?

Why didn't she call out? Surely she would if she was frightened.

It was almost as if she had expected—*nonsense!*

A light flashed above his head. He was starting to get up, one hand on the carpeted floor, but the light dazzled him and he dropped flat again, keeping his head up so that his chin wouldn't bang against the floor. Slowly he looked up from under his eyebrows.

'*You!*' he gasped.

A woman was sitting up in bed. She wore a flimsy nightdress with a deep V which did little to conceal her large, pale bosom. She was blonde. Her lips were still bright with yesterday's lipstick—crimson red, which he had seen at the magistrate's court when she had given evidence.

For this was Maisie Dunster, and she was covering him with a small pistol, a pistol which, if loaded, could kill.

She sat rigidly, mouth set in a rounded 'Oh'. The gun was steady in her right hand. Her left was behind her, and she was using it to support herself against the pillows. Her eyes, though heavy from sleep, were almost as rounded as her lips.

Very slowly, Roger began to get up. The humiliation itself wasn't very important, the ache in his side wasn't either; drawing up first one knee, then the other, he supported himself with one hand on the floor. He was perhaps six feet away from the side of the bed, the door immediately behind him.

Maisie licked her lips, then said in a husky voice, 'Don't come any nearer.'

He began to get up.

'Sit on the floor,' she ordered.

If he obeyed, then he would not only be helpless but she would have the upper hand morally, as well as with the threat of the gun. There were some things one did almost instinctively, and he did one now.

He stood up.

He knew, with half of his mind, that she might shoot him, but he was driven by a compulsion which made him take the chance. He felt giddy once he was on his feet, and his knees bent. He lurched towards the bed, and Maisie thrust the pistol out farther. Lurching backwards, quite unavoidably, he struck the front edge of a chair with the back of his knees, and dropped into it, helplessly. It was heavy and padded and although it swayed to and fro a few inches it didn't topple backwards and he didn't fall.

'My God!' she exclaimed. 'It *is* you!'

He gulped.

'West,' he admitted. 'Superintendent West. I have—' He broke off. He had been about to add that he had a search warrant, but in these circumstances it would sound absurd.

Maisie Dunster shifted her position, hitching the pillow up behind her, and adjusting the neck of her nightdress.

'What the hell are you doing here?' she asked gustily.

West hesitated. Whatever else, she showed no venom and no malice, and the simple truth should be as good an answer as any. He shifted his position to ease the ache in his back, and answered, 'I came to search the room.'

'Why?'

'It's occupied by—' He stopped abruptly, then forced a grin. 'I *thought* it was occupied by a Mr. Patrick Fogarty.'

'Well,' she said, 'he pays the rent.'

Roger was feeling much more composed, even grateful to the girl for not giving him the run around when it would have been so easy to have made him feel still more of a fool than he looked.

'And you accept his hospitality on occasions,' he remarked.

Her eyes gleamed with a hint of humour, but he didn't expect the retort she gave.

'On those nights when I'm not one of four in a bed,' she said. 'Funny you should guess about the foursome, Mr. West.'

'Very funny,' said West dryly, 'if there *was* a foursome on that particular night.'

Maisie leant forward, still gripping the gun.

'Let me tell you something, Mr. West: nothing is going to make me say I wasn't with Mario last night. Or the night before last, whenever it was. And if I like to spend one night with one boy friend and the next with another and then have a free-for-all, it's nothing to do with you or the Police Force, the Bishop of Canterbury or God, for that matter. I'm myself, you understand. I do what I like with myself, and I go with anyone I like.' Then, she broke off, frowning. 'What do you want at Fogarty's, anyhow?'

'He killed a man last night,' stated Roger.

She was so shocked that he thought he had a chance to throw himself forward and disarm her, and but for the pain in his ribs he might have tried. But even when he shifted forward, it shot up to his shoulder and down to his knee.

'You bloody liar!' she burst out. 'Pat wouldn't hurt—!'

'He ran the man down on a zebra crossing,' explained Roger. 'He didn't run away and there's a possibility that he was drunk.' Her face began to clear as if she were prepared to accept that as a possibility, but he brought a frown back almost instantly by going on, 'His victim was one of the two witnesses against Mario Rapelli. Isn't that a remarkable coincidence?'

The effect of his words was so great that she leant back against the pillow, almost dropping the gun. He felt quite sure that it would be safe to get up and cross to her— but as he began, putting most of his weight on the left leg, which hadn't been hurt, there was a sharp tap at the door.

Chapter Seven

DISASTER?

The girl started, and slowly raised her gun again. Roger looked towards the door, and his heart began to thump. Who was the caller? It was bad enough already, but if someone else saw him in here there would be two witnesses. He put his left hand on the arm of the chair, to hoist himself up.

'Who's there?' Maisie called out.

'It's no one you know,' a man replied. 'Is West still there?'

She hesitated, and then asked, 'Who's West?'

'Don't play tricks, Maisie. Is he there?'

She pursed her lips but didn't answer and it was almost possible to guess what she was thinking: which would be the greatest fun, to admit that he was still here, or to pretend that he had gone.

'Maisie,' the man said in a harsh voice, 'you could get hurt—or you could be richer by a hundred pounds.'

Her eyes narrowed, and she said, 'That's *money*.'

'You're right, it's money. Cash money.'

'What do I have to do?'

'Is West still there?'

'What do I have to do?' she insisted.

There was a pause and a whisper of voices came from the other side of the door. So at least two men were out there. The whispering did not last long, and the first man spoke again, urgency in his voice.

'Maisie, listen. I want a few pictures of you and Handsome West in bed together. That's all. You don't have to do a thing except undress. You've got him covered, haven't you? You've got a gun.'

'I've got a gun and I'm covering him with it,' Maisie answered.

'So there's no problem,' the man called. 'Make him undress and get into bed with you. Then I'll come in and take a few pretty pictures. And you can have the hundred smackers *now*.' There was a short pause before he went on, 'Here's some proof, Maisie. Look under the door.'

Maisie's gaze dropped to the door.

For a split second, Roger glanced towards the door, also. And immediately paper showed, as if it had been at floor level ready to slip beneath the bottom of the door. The first glimpse showed it for a five pound note, and after it was right inside the room, a second followed it.

Roger looked away from the money to Maisie, and he saw the expression on her face. There was tightness— avarice?—at her mouth and a mean look in her eyes. She actually licked her lips as she glanced at Roger. The rustling of the currency notes sounded quite clearly in a silence otherwise broken only by their breathing.

The man called, 'That's thirty quid, Maisie.'

'Show some more.' Maisie's voice was tense.

'Thirty's a good earnest.'

'I want to see sixty.'

'But—'

'If you haven't got it, forget it. No one's going to leave here until I've seen the colour of sixty quid. Mr. Superintendent Roger West or anyone. Show the money.'

There was only a short pause before more money came

through the gap at the foot of the door. It was in one pound notes now, quite a sheaf of them at a time. Maisie looked at Roger, the gun steady in her hand, and pointing towards his stomach. He had a feeling that she had used a gun before and would unhesitatingly use one again.

'Okay, peeler,' she said to Roger. 'Peel.'

The man outside crowed, 'That's my baby!'

'Peel, peeler.' Maisie played on the word again, obviously pleased with her joke. 'It's not so difficult. I know a lot of men who would jump at the chance of getting in bed with me.' When Roger didn't even begin to move, she went on in a sharper voice, 'Do what I tell you!'

Roger stood up, slowly. He felt as if he were a character in a film or television series; not quite real. The situation was as bizarre as any he had experienced; and in its way, as deadly. So was Maisie Dunster. From the way she handled the pistol he felt even more sure that she was used to it, and from the set of her lips he felt nearly sure that she would shoot unless he obeyed. But he couldn't possibly obey. He couldn't in any circumstances allow himself to be photographed, naked, in bed with this woman. Nothing would ever explain it away. His reputation would be smashed. Coppell would have to suspend him from duty and at the very best he would have to resign.

For the first time he recalled the luncheon date with Benjamin Artemeus, and he almost grinned.

'Take that grin off your face and get a move on,' she ordered; and she touched the trigger.

The report of the shot was very sharp, making Roger start. He heard the bullet smack into the wall behind him; it could not have missed his face by more than an inch. After the thud of sound there was utter silence for several seconds, and during them Roger found a hundred thoughts flashing through his mind, none of them pleasant.

There wasn't an iota of doubt left about Maisie's seriousness. If he started to undress, she might relax, but it wasn't likely; she had a very wary glint in her eyes.

If by some miracle he got out of this room, then there were the men on the landing to stop him.

'Handsome,' she said, levelling the gun at his middle, 'I'm not going to tell you again. Strip!'

He unbuttoned his jacket, took it off slowly, and draped it over the arm of the big chair. He unbuttoned his waistcoat with slow deliberation, and did the same with that. He put his hand to the knot of his tie and as he undid it took a step towards the bed. His side still hurt, but not so much. He let the ends of the tie dangle loose, and then spoke for the first time.

'You're crazy to do this.'

'So I'm crazy.'

'It couldn't be worth it for a thousand pounds, let alone a hundred.'

'You ought to look in my handbag,' she said. 'Hurry.'

'Maisie,' the man from outside called. 'How about opening the door so that we can help you?'

'He'll open the door when he's ready,' Maisie called back. 'I don't trust you any more than I trust him.'

'Maisie,' Roger said, 'you'll have every policeman at the Yard after you.'

'And you'll have every policeman at the Yard laughing at you,' Maisie jeered. 'Those photographs will be worth a fortune. I can sell my life story to any Sunday newspaper! Hurry.'

He sprang at her from a standing start.

He knew that she had time to squeeze the trigger, that at point blank range she couldn't miss. He could be killed; badly wounded; blinded. But there was no time to find out. He heard the bark of the shot, felt burning on his cheek, then closed with her, gripping her right wrist and thrusting it sideways, flinging his right arm round her and hugging her close. Her body, except at the breasts, was very firm, and he felt her arms tighten as big muscles flexed. As she began to struggle he realised that unless he finished this quickly, he could be in deepest trouble. There was a momentary reluctance to fight as if she were a man, until he felt her knee driving against his thigh; an inch or two to the right and he would be in agony.

So he chopped the side of his right hand down on to the back of her neck. Locks of hair took some of the force of the blow but it nearly knocked her out, and she sagged away from him. He let her fall back. She wasn't faking, she was almost out. Dragging her down towards the foot of the bed, he rolled her up in the bedclothes, leaving only her head and face and her feet showing.

The man outside called, 'Maisie!' in an urgent voice.

Roger raised his voice in a gasping falsetto.

'Coming!' he called.

He bent down and picked up the pistol, went to the door, which had a Yale lock and, when slammed, was self-locking and could only be opened from the outside with the key. He turned the knob slowly, then jerked the door open. He saw one man disappearing down the stairs. He fired a shot over the man's head, bringing him to a shocked standstill, his thin face turning towards Roger.

The other was halfway down the second flight of stairs, still moving. Roger fired a shot which struck the stairs just ahead of him, and he also came to a standstill, slipped on a stair and nearly fell. He grabbed the banister rail to save himself. He didn't turn round but there was a familiar look about him.

'Stay there,' Roger ordered. He started down, pushed past the small man who now cowered against the wall.

The other was pressing against the wall, too, his gaze on Roger's gun.

That was the moment when Roger recognised him: he was the pastry-cook from Bethnal Green—Hamish Campbell!

Roger, gun in hand, pushed past him. As he did so a door downstairs opened and a Jamaican girl came out, brightly dressed and attractive. She glanced up in surprise at the sight of Roger.

He smiled broadly, reassuringly, and asked, 'Will you call the police, please? Dial 999 and ask for the police service and ask them to send a car here at once. Give them the number of the street, will you?'

'Why, surely,' she gasped. 'Of course I will.' She hurried to the pre-payment telephone in the hall and glanced round, opening her bag. She kept her head very well and there was only the faintest of quivers in her voice.

It was while she was talking that Roger felt wave after wave of relief surge over him.

Three minutes later, a police car arrived.

'I'll charge these two men with uttering threats and common assault,' Roger said to the police from the car. 'Watch the big one very carefully.'

'Are we to take them to division?' the patrol officer asked.

'Yes,' Roger said. 'Then send for a car with a woman officer; there's a woman upstairs we want to take in— "uttering threats" will do to start with on her. Don't lose any time, will you?'

'Not a split second, sir,' the other assured him.

In twenty minutes Maisie Dunster was on her way to divisional headquarters in a police car, and the two men were ahead of her. Roger did not follow, but went to the Yard, arriving about ten o'clock. He went straight to his office, nodding right and left but acutely aware of the

fact that his arrival was receiving more than the usual
attention. There were several messages on his desk, including one reading: *Please call the commander*. It was
timed at nine-five over an hour ago. He put in the call
at once and Coppell's secretary spoke with a note of
malice in her voice.

'The commander is *very* late for a conference, waiting
for you.' There was a moment's pause before Coppell
growled, 'Come and see me, *now*.'

Roger was at the outer office door a few minutes later,
glanced at the secretary, who set her lips thinly and led
the way to the communicating door. She opened it and
Roger went through, to see Coppell putting down a
telephone. He glowered up.

'Where the hell have you been?'

For a split second, Roger felt the familiar anger rising,
but he couldn't reasonably blame Coppell for his own
mood or his own folly. A phrase came into his head and
almost before he realised he was going to utter it, he
blurted, 'Getting myself in more trouble.'

That stopped even Coppell, whose lips parted—and
then closed as he sat back heavily in his chair.

'Come again?'

'I went to search the room of the driver of the car with
which our witness Smithson was killed. I made another
mistake.' Coppell was still so taken aback that he missed
the obvious: *'another'*, and Roger went on, 'I took it for
granted that it would be empty. Instead, a woman was
there, and a couple of bright sparks offered her a hundred
quid to take me to bed—at the point of a gun.' Roger
paused, then took the pistol out of his pocket. 'Here's the
gun,' he said, and placed it in front of Coppell. 'It came
near to killing me.'

Coppell was staring at him incredulously, and Roger
realised that he was gazing particularly at his right cheek.

Almost mechanically, Roger put his hand up to his face, and he touched a sore spot, looked at his fingers and saw a smear of blood.

'So they came as near as that,' Coppell said, no longer angry or growling. 'Would you recognise them again?'

'They're all at division, on a charge,' Roger said flatly.

'Who was with you?' Coppell asked.

Roger thought: Here it comes. It was an effort to answer, 'No one.'

Coppell gasped, 'You went *alone?*'

'Yes, sir.'

'Well, no one could ever question your guts whatever they might say about your sense.' Coppell gave a twisted grin which robbed the words of most of their sting. 'I have to go and report to the commissioner. If it goes right, this little job might save your bacon.' With a flare of alarm, he asked, 'They didn't get a photograph, did they?'

'No. And I didn't get into bed,' Roger retorted.

Coppell sniffed back a laugh. 'Almost a pity you didn't,' he rasped. 'You really would be the playboy of the Yard, then, wouldn't you?' He stood up.

Roger answered, straight-faced, 'Yes, sir. The woman was Maisie Dunster.'

'Maisie—' Coppell was completely taken aback again. 'That witness for Rapelli, you mean? The alibi bedfellow?' There was a hint of a stutter in his voice.

'Yes,' answered Roger.

'And she was in the room of the man who ran down and killed a witness *against* Rapelli. My God! We've got some strings to unravel here,' Coppell declared. 'What about our second witness? Don't let anything happen to him, will you? If you do I'll have your neck.'

'I've taken very good care of him,' Roger said confidently. 'He's the man who wanted Maisie to pop into bed with me while he took some photographs. What did you say about strings to unravel?'

He did not believe that he had ever seen the commander so dumbfounded, utterly bereft of words. It seemed a long time before Coppell began to relax, and as he did so the communicating door opened and his secretary said in a reproving voice, 'The commissioner has just called again. He insisted—' She broke off, astounded at Coppell's expression.

Very slowly the commander of the Criminal Investigations Department stood up. He rounded his desk and was halfway to the door before he turned round, saying gruffly, 'Better come with me, Handsome. The commissioner had better hear this straight from the horse's mouth.'

Chapter Eight

DISAPPROVAL

The commissioner of the Metropolitan Police, Sir Jacob Trevillion, was a big, bucolic man, ex-navy, with a manner too often faintly reminiscent of a drill-sergeant. He had a saving sense of humour, his bark being always worse than his bite, and he overlooked a great many errors provided rules and regulations were strictly observed. Entering his office, these things passed through Roger's mind and he even wondered whether Coppell could have brought him along here on the 'it's time West was taught a lesson' principle. He had never met this man face to face over Yard business, only on official and social occasions, and he felt a sharp sense of trepidation.

In front of the commissioner was a copy of last night's *Globe*.

He was frowning; and after a swift glance towards them he put the newspaper to one side and shuffled through some papers. Roger saw that amongst them were some of his own and some of Coppell's reports on the Rapelli case.

The commissioner kept them standing just long enough to make Roger begin to fret, then looked up once more.

'Ah, commander. Have a seat. Superintendent—I think you have some explanations to make.'

Roger said in a flat voice, 'About what, sir?'

'About your grave error of judgment when you asked a question in court yesterday.'

Roger kept silent.

'Well?' the commissioner barked.

'I don't really think I committed an error of judgment, sir.'

'You don't *what*! When this—' the commissioner placed a fist on the *Globe* '—so severely takes *you* and the Yard to task!'

'I know I asked for trouble, sir, but it was an odd situation, and got out of hand. I felt it essential to establish the character of the witness who really shouldn't have been allowed to testify. Thanks to some very clever tactics by her counsel, she was being allowed to give evidence that she had been in bed with a man accused of a serious crime, at the time of the crime. If it ever came to trial, as I would expect, this evidence would be on record. I did take a chance, sir, in establishing her character—'

'That's enough, Superintendent.'

'Sir.'

'You've been in the service long enough to know the elementary rules, haven't you?' The sarcasm almost dripped.

'Yes, sir,' Roger said, very quietly. 'I have been in the Force for twenty-six years. And in countless cases I have managed to get results by taking some risks. Once that alibi evidence was given, the damage was done, and I felt impelled to try to discredit the witness. The very fact that a junior partner of a highly reputable firm of solicitors—'

'*That's enough, West!*' roared the commissioner. 'Rules are rules, and by God I'll have you know it!'

'Commissioner,' Coppell interrupted, in a strangely mild voice for him, 'West found the girl witness in another man's bed this morning. The bed of a man who ran down and killed one of the prosecution's witnesses in the Rapelli case.'

The commissioner stared, his lips parted; his expression one of complete bafflement. Coppell, having said his piece, crossed his thick legs and fell silent. Roger felt an unexpected surge of appreciation, of gratitude; but he was far from being out of the wood yet. He would have to be extremely careful what he said and how he said it; the trouble was that although he knew he had stuck his neck out and that the commissioner's manner wasn't at all unjustified, he himself was seething with resentment, and it would be difficult to keep a hold on his tongue. He tried to relax—eyes, lips, set of his chin and shoulders, but the effort wasn't very successful.

Then he saw the change of expression in the commissioner's eyes. An 'I've got him' look which he had seen in the eyes of senior officers often, when he had been younger. He steeled himself for whatever was coming.

'You *found* the girl in another man's bed?'

'Yes, sir.'

'In his bedroom, presumably.'

'Yes, sir.'

'Was she asleep? Awake? Was the man with her?'

'She was alone, sir.'

'And how many police officers did you have with you?'

'None, sir.'

'Ah.' The commissioner looked triumphant. 'The girl was in bed—by herself?'

'Yes, sir.'

'And you were in the room, unaccompanied by any police officers.'

'Yes, sir.'

'Was *anyone* with you?'

'No, sir,' Roger stated. 'Two men, one a photographer,

were in the passage outside.'

The commissioner rode that like a cruiser riding an Atlantic wave; he ignored it.

'Was the door locked or unlocked?'

'Locked, sir.'

'I see, Superintendent. You, a police officer—' He gulped. 'Did you have a warrant to search the room?'

'Yes, sir.'

'Had you been freely *admitted* to this young woman's room?'

'No, sir,' Roger said very stiffly. His mouth was dry, his temper high, and his heart was in his boots. The commissioner was conducting this examination as if it were a court-martial, and it was not material that this kind of aggressive questioning was almost unique—that a commissioner might be called upon to decide on what kind of disciplinary action should be taken was permissible, but such direct participation was unheard of.

'So,' said the commissioner, looking at Coppell. 'Not satisfied with a public display of questionable behaviour, you entered a room occupied by a young lady unbidden and alone. Commander, I propose to suspend Superintendent West from duty for an indefinite period, until in fact his conduct of this case can be fully investigated.'

Roger clenched his teeth, and met the older man's gaze when it switched back to him. Coppell caught his breath with a curiously choking noise. Roger waited for dismissal, still not saying a word. If he once opened his lips a torrent would spill out.

'Ach—sir,' Coppell choked.

'Yes, Commander?'

'West was—ah—shot at.'

'By the woman?'

'Yes, sir.'

'Don't I understand that the laws of this country make

it justifiable to shoot or otherwise attack an intruder *in his own home*?'

'Yes, sir, but—'

'Shall we discuss this matter in private, Commander?'

'Ah—if you say so, sir. But I think it would be a great disservice to suspend Superintendent West at this juncture.'

Roger was as astounded as the commissioner, who obviously could not believe his ears. He turned open-mouthed towards Coppell, who was now on his feet. And Roger, glancing at Coppell, saw a beading of perspiration at his forehead and upper lip, although it was not really hot in here.

'Indeed,' the commissioner said. 'Wait outside, Superintendent,' he added to Roger.

Roger drew a very deep breath, turned smartly, and went towards the door. He did not glance at Coppell, but went out, closing the door softly behind him.

He was in a passage in an unfamiliar part of the new Yard building. This was the Administrative Section, where C.I.D. men seldom came, and he had not been here before. The passage was wide, the floor carpeted, the walls panelled. There were chairs and couches, all of brown leather. He moistened his lips and wished above all things for a drink, but there was not even a cloakroom in sight. He walked stiffly to the end of the passage and saw a door marked *Gentlemen*. He went in, and found paper cups and a drinking-fountain. He rinsed his mouth with cold water several times, then drank a little before returning to the other passage. The commissioner's door was still closed, he hadn't been gone for three minutes. He began to walk up and down, stiffly; began feeling again. He had been quite numbed. Shock, of course. Shock, and repressed resentment and anger. The commissioner had behaved like the governor of a prison rather than the Chief of Police.

Well—what *had* he done?

There wasn't any argument about it, though: by going to that room and using the key and entering by himself, he had driven roughshod over regulations. Even though, had the room been empty, there would have been no trouble, he was still in the wrong, and he couldn't really blame the commissioner for saying so.

Two men and a girl passed, all of them startled at the sight of him; C.I.D. men were not here often. They went on. He could hear nothing from the commissioner's room and began to wonder how Coppell was doing. Coppell was obviously in awe of the commissioner but he had put up a fight. Good God! What was happening to the Yard to have a man at its head who could cow a commander of one of the departments!

Without warning, the door opened, and Coppell stood there, a pale-faced Coppell, who licked his lips before he said, 'Come in.'

There was nothing in his expression to tell Roger what had happened. Roger had an almost overwhelming temptation to turn and walk away. Better anything than face such an indignity. No, no, no, that was crazy thinking. He must face the situation ... Good Lord! He had a luncheon appointment with Benjamin Artemeus about a possible new job. The thought was like a shot in the arm, and must have shown in his face and his manner as he went in.

The commissioner was standing up; was that a concession?

Roger stopped a few feet away from him, and waited.

'Superintendent,' said the commissioner, 'I am given to understand that you have made considerable progress in the current investigation. Further, I am aware that there were extenuating circumstances to your gross failure to observe regulations. In these circumstances the matter of suspension is held over. I want you to understand, however, that the rules and regulations of the Force *must* be observed.' He paused, and then barked, 'Do you understand?'

A wave of relief greater than he had ever known surged over Roger as he answered, 'Perfectly, sir.'

'Very well,' said the commissioner, and nodded dismissal.

*   *   *

'That was bloody purgatory,' Coppell growled.

Roger swallowed hard.

'Thanks for what you did.'

'The man's a—' began Coppell, only to break off. 'Can't say you helped yourself much.'

'I got off on the wrong foot,' Roger said.

'Yes. Better watch your feet.'

'I certainly will,' Roger said feelingly.

They walked along in silence for some time, until they were in the C.I.D. building, passing familiar places and familiar faces. Then Coppell shot Roger a sidelong look, and said, 'Bloody unfortunate. I tried—'

He was outside his office and his secretary appeared, a wild look in her eyes. She glared at Roger as she spoke to Coppell.

'Sir, your call to Vienna has come through. I've been trying everywhere to find you.'

'Didn't have far to look,' grunted Coppell, and nodded to West. 'See you.'

He went into his office and the door closed. For a few seconds Roger was in the passage alone and it reminded him vividly of waiting outside the commissioner's room. Well, he hadn't been suspended, and he could carry on with the case, but—oh, to hell with it all! The pressures were too great.

He felt heavy-hearted and dismayed, both at himself and what had followed. Not only did this case seem to have gremlins working against him, but he was making his own gremlins. He hadn't had time to think about it last night because of Scoop's problem and he hadn't allowed himself time to think this morning. He glanced at his watch, and saw that it was twenty past twelve. If he were going to that lunch he would have to get a move on; he would be at least ten minutes late as it was. He opened the door of his own office and went inside, and as he did so Danizon appeared at the communicating door.

Danizon smiled, the most normal and trouble-free sight Roger had seen that morning.

'Just looked in to remind you about your luncheon appointment,' he said. 'A Mr. Artemeus rang up ten minutes ago. I promised to ring him at the Savoy Grill if you couldn't make it.'

'Ring and tell him I'll be twenty minutes late,' Roger ordered.

*　　*　　*

The luxury and the ostentation of the Savoy Grill was more than a change, it was a salve and a solace. So was being recognised by the doorman and one of the porters, and by the head waiter when he went in.

'Ah, Superintendent West—Mr. Artemeus is here.' He led the way to a corner table at which there was room for four but where one man was waiting. This could only be Artemeus. He was a heavily-built, beautifully groomed man, probably in the middle-fifties, with a somewhat sallow complexion and iron-grey hair. As Roger appeared he stood up, hand outstretched.

'Mr. West. How good of you to come.'

'Thank you for the invitation,' Roger said, gripping firmly and finding that Artemeus's grip was also firm but not over-hearty. The head waiter pulled the table out for Roger to sit down, and another waiter hovered.

'What will you have?' asked Artemeus.

'A whisky and soda, please.'

'And bring me another pink gin,' Artemeus ordered the second waiter. When they were alone he proffered cigarettes, and Roger took one almost with relief. He seldom smoked these days, but this might help a little to ease tension.

'Thanks.'

Artemeus said, almost warily, 'Dare I say you look a little worn, Mr. West?'

Roger half-laughed.

'More than a little,' he said. 'I've had a rough morning.'

'One of the—ah—problems you face, no doubt, is the sudden pressure of work, both day and night,' said Artemeus, smiling deprecatingly. 'And one of the advantages I can offer you are regular hours, excellent working conditions, and—but perhaps you would prefer to wait until we've had lunch before we get to the crux of the matter.'

The waiter arrived with the drinks at almost miraculous speed, and put them down. Roger picked up his glass.

'Cheers.'

'Cheers.'

'Ah! That's good,' Roger said, and sipped again. 'I think I could bear to hear whatever you want to say, then I can ponder and we can perhaps discuss it over luncheon.'

'Good, good!' approved Artemeus. 'Oh—I took the liberty of ordering smoked salmon and saddle of lamb— I hope you approve. If not, of course, the menu—'

'Both sound just right,' Roger said, and sipped again.

'Splendid!' Artemeus was just a little over-hearty, over-emphatic, over-anxious to please. 'Very well, then, I will get straight to the point. I am a director of Allsafe, the second largest firm of security police in the country, Mr. West. We have some excellent men in all departments and a very extensive business; there is so much in industrial security which the existing police forces cannot handle.' He paused as if to give Roger a chance to comment but Roger simply nodded non-committally. 'We need an administrator to replace one who is shortly to retire, and we want an experienced, highly successful detective from Scotland Yard. With such a man at our head we would greatly impress not only our present clients but also attract many new ones. You are the man we want. There is no better-known policeman, none who attracts so much public attention, or, may I say, approval. We would, of course, pay a salary fully commensurate with your reputation and your position—'

Artemeus paused for a long time and his gaze was very intent; even piercing. Then he went on with great deliberation, 'The salary would be twenty thousand pounds a year—that is, some four times your present emolument. And if that is not sufficient inducement by itself, then perhaps the prospect of a carte blanche on expenses and six weeks holiday a year, including this year if you could join us so quickly, would make the offer more attractive.'

He sat back and sipped his pink gin, while Roger reacted to what he had said in utter disbelief.

Chapter Nine

QUESTIONS

Roger was aware of the chatter of conversation about him, the clatter of dishes, of distant music. An attractive brunette in a wide-brimmed hat, sitting at a table near-by, was obviously more intrigued by him than by her companion. The waiter came up, enquiringly, and Artemeus asked, 'Another Scotch, Mr. West?'

'Er—no, thanks.'

'Then we'll have the wine,' declared Artemeus. 'And tell M'sieu Henri we will start luncheon.'

'Very good, sir.'

As the waiter disappeared, deftly weaving his way between tables, Artemeus turned back to Roger with a faint smile, and finished his drink. Roger downed his. He was almost sure that that woman in the wide-brimmed hat was trying to flirt with him; certainly she was trying to attract and hold his attention. In a way he was glad she was there; he could glance at her from time to time and so hide his astonishment at the hugeness of the offer.

Artemeus was obviously waiting for him to comment.

'That's a very large sum of money,' Roger remarked at last.

'It is a reasonable sum in commercial circles but very substantial compared with the salaries of civil servants,' Artemeus replied. 'I have always believed that senior civil servants, particularly the police, have been scandalously underpaid.' Roger let that go without comment. 'The private security organisations are better off, especially among the higher ranks, of course.'

'Or you wouldn't get them to leave the London and provincial forces,' remarked Roger drily. 'How did the men who came to you from the ex-colonies shape up?'

'Very well, on the whole,' Artemeus told him.

As he spoke, a black-suited, black-tied waiter with an aproned youth to wait on him appeared with a dish of Scotch smoked salmon and paper-thin brown bread and butter. Roger waited until they had both been served before he asked, 'What makes you think my publicity value is worth so much?'

'Simple power of observation,' answered Artemeus smoothly.

'Doesn't that put you on the spot?' asked Roger.

'Meaning?'

'That I could ask for more.'

Artemeus pursed his lips.

'How much more?'

'I haven't even begun to think it through,' answered Roger. 'In fact the offer you'd made would be big enough if I were of a mind to resign from the Yard.'

'Are you?' asked Artemeus, quite sharply.

'I can't really say I am,' answered Roger slowly, 'but I can't truthfully say that I don't sometimes get tired of the Yard.' He shrugged. 'The hours, the fact that one is constantly on call—'

'The fact that your wife gets sick of being disappointed when, instead of taking her out, you're called to a job,' Artemeus murmured. 'West, I don't want to try to persuade you, and I don't for a moment expect an immediate answer now. I can leave the offer open for two months, perhaps a little more, to the end of July. If you haven't accepted by then, I'll have to look for someone else.'

He stopped, while the saddle of lamb, beautifully browned, was brought to them on a large copper dish and then carved at their side. There were green peas mixed with tiny onions, new potatoes and mint sauce with redcurrant jelly. After they were served, he continued as if there had been no pause.

'Meanwhile, I'll be glad to answer any questions, now or later.'

'Thank you,' Roger said. 'First—is the offer confidential?'

'Absolutely. Only my board and I know about it. All discussion has been in person, and none of my staff has been involved.'

'Thanks. Where would the job be?'

'You would be in London most of the time and your office and staff would be situated centrally. There are five provincial or regional offices and you would probably need to visit two of them each month.'

'What kind of work is involved?'

'Industrial and commercial security, such as watching buildings—particularly banks, conveying wages from banks to factories and offices, investigating industrial sabotage of all kinds. You would find it a cake-walk, West.'

'Possibly,' Roger said drily. 'What staff would I have?'

'You would need at least two secretaries, probably two receptionists and some other clerical help.'

'About three times what I get now,' Roger said ruefully.

'Precisely. You could do your job of organising a nationwide security service, instead of spending half your time making out reports, talking to subordinates and kow-towing to the com—' Artemeus broke off, looking slyly at Roger. 'I'm sorry,' he added mockingly, 'I quite forgot. You aren't exactly the type to kow-tow to any-one, are you?'

Roger said evasively, 'I have my superiors.'

'Yes, indeed. Well!' Artemeus beckoned the waiter and pointed to the saddle of lamb, now beneath the huge lid. 'Another two cuts, I think,' he said, 'and the rest for Mr. West.' After the carving and the fussing was over and the table wheeled away, he went on, 'Any more quesitons?'

'No pressing ones,' Roger answered.

'Good! So far you've come up with nothing I wasn't prepared for.' Artemeus went on eating, and then said a-propos of nothing, 'Your no doubt revered chief used to come in here quite a lot, before he became your chief. *Is* he doing the job he was supposed to do?'

Roger asked guardedly, 'Which particular chief?'

'Oh, the comissioner: Sir Jacob Trevillion.'

'I didn't know he'd been appointed to do any particular job,' Roger replied. 'I don't move in such exalted circles.'

'Oh.' Artemeus seemed surprised, but Roger doubted whether he really was. 'Well, rumour has it that discipline at the Yard was getting slack and needed tightening. Trevillion was a martinet—stickler for discipline—in the Navy. He—'

'You know, I'm not sure that I want to discuss him,' Roger interrupted.

'Oh, I'm sorry. I didn't intend—' Artemeus broke off, as if in confusion, but after a few minutes he turned to another subject, broaching it with a self-deprecatory smile. 'I don't suppose you're able to discuss a case you're work-ing on, either. It is an unusual one you've got now, isn't it?'

'You mean, the death of the man Verdi.'

'Yes. And the bosomy blonde whom you so nicely dealt with in court,' added Artemeus. 'I'm less interested in the victim and his assailant and the witnesses, though, than

I am in Rachel Warrender. You know, the girl solicitor who appeared for Rapelli at the last moment.' He looked hard at Roger, who nodded, and then went on, 'She's a remarkable young woman from a remarkable family. Do you know much about Warrender, Clansel and Warrender?'

'Not much,' said Roger, still guardedly; but now his interest was increasing swiftly. A question was banging against his mind like a trip-hammer. Could this be what Artemeus had really wanted to see him about, or was the mention of the girl simply fortuitous? He had wondered at the timing of the offer, and the ingenuous way in which Artemeus had brought the commissioner into the conversation had been worth noting. Now here was 'coincidence' number two.

'They're mostly insurance and banking lawyers,' said the other man. 'It's fourth generation in each family. Sir Ian Warrender, the senior partner, probably knows more about international insurance and banking laws than anyone alive. He received his knighthood for services in connection with the Bank of England's overseas activities. Jonathan Clansel was a channel swimmer—did it both ways—and is a great supporter of Boysland.' Boysland, West recollected, was a very big youth club, or group of clubs, which operated mostly in the East End of London. 'Sir Roland Warrender, bother of Sir Ian, who also got his knighthood for banking activities—' Artemeus broke off with a smile, then asked, 'Ring a bell?'

'Sir Roland Warrender, the Member of Parliament who's so right-wing the Conservative Party disowned him last year?' asked Roger.

'Yes. He's Rachel's father.'

'So I understand.'

'She's a junior partner. Older than she looks.' went on Artemeus. 'In her late twenties. I was surprised at first

that they'd allowed her to intervene for Rapelli, but the
more I think of it, the more reasonable it seems. She
doesn't fit in with the family party line. She's extremely
left-wing, a great campaigner for anti-Vietnam, anti-
colonialism of any kind, anti-nuclear weapons, anti—' He
broke off with a smile. 'She's like the rest of the family in
do-gooding and looking out for the underdog—but she
sometimes gets a bit confused as to who the underdog is,'
he added drily. 'How did she show up in court?'

'Very well, I would say.'

'Clever—I *mean* clever—girl,' opined Artemeus. 'I can
see her as a Member of Parliament one of these days,
campaigning for votes for babies at the breast!' He
beckoned the waiter. 'How about a dessert, Mr. West?
They do a very good chocolate gateau here, or their trifles
are excellent.'

'I think cheese—'

'I'm for the gateau,' Artemeus declared. 'And coffee?
How about brandy or a liqueur?'

'I have to work this afternoon,' Roger protested, half-
laughing.

'Wait until you work for us,' Artemeus said slyly. 'Then
you can take three hours for a big business lunch, and
have an hour's nap before you have to wake up to go
home!'

*   *   *

Where was the catch? wondered Roger. There must be
one. He couldn't possibly consider the offer on its face
value.

*   *   *

As he walked out of the hotel into the bright sunshine

of one of the warmest days of summer, Roger saw a nearly
empty number 11 bus which would drop him within a
minute's walk of Broadway and the Yard's new home. He
needed a little time for reflection and to recover from the
enormous meal. Hastily buying a copy of the latest *Globe*,
he boarded the bus, hurried up the stairs, and stumbled
towards a vacant bench at the front, head bent low to
avoid the roof. For a few minutes he sat looking through
the window as the panorama first of the Strand, then of
Trafalgar Square, opened out in front of him, followed
by the tall and graceful buildings of Whitehall.

At last, he opened the newspaper.

Death of Trial Witness screamed the first headline.
Arrest of Another ran the second.

There was a fairly accurate account of the death of
Wilfred Smithson and another of the arrest of Maisie
Dunster, some reference to West but no sneers or
innuendo, only a slightly critical tone about the Yard's
'carelessness' in allowing a witness to be run down.
Roger folded the paper and put it under his arm, almost
as the bus passed the narrow end of the street which led
down to the old building of Scotland Yard. He had a
great nostalgia for the red-brick edifice in which he
had spent most of his working life, but when he reached
the new headquarters, he could not fail to compare its
lightness and airiness favourably.

He went in, at exactly half past three.

He had a strange feeling as he walked along the plain,
almost hospital-like passage to his office—a feeling which
was almost a dread of trouble, of complaint and accusation. But everything was normal, including a note on his
desk from Danizon.

'I'm in Records—back by 3.45 p.m.'

He would be, too.

Roger sat at his desk and looked at the files in front

of him, each with a copy of his own report, each with
contributions from divisional officers, detective sergeants,
uniform, policewomen, the Flying Squad, Fingerprints,
Records, Photography, Information, pathologists, doctors,
coroners, and police courts. There they were, making the
whole routine of an investigation. In one of these was the
investigation into the death of Ricardo Verdi. Before this
case was closed that particular file would be inches thick,
hundreds upon hundreds of pages, two, three, four
volumes.

The one on Maisie Dunster would be pretty fat, too.

So would that on Rapelli himself, as well as the one on
Fogarty, Smithson and Campbell.

In a way every word was necessary, but at times even
thought and sight of them flooded West with irritation.

Quite suddenly, the full significance of Artemeus's
offer swept over him. He could be free from all this
ponderous, inescapable routine; he could have four times
the money to spend, regular hours, guaranteed holidays.
He could begin a whole new life, live in a whole new
world. For a few moments he sat back, basking in the
promised sun. Then, sharply, he sat up. Maisie and
Fogarty had had time to think, it was past time he went
to question them again.

Neither had yet made any statement of any kind.

He read the list of the contents in their pockets and in
Maisie's handbag, briefed himself completely and then
telephoned the Fulham Police Station.

'I'm coming over right away,' he told the inspector-in-
charge.

'It can't be too soon, sir,' the man said. 'That Dunster
woman is a proper harridan. Talk about language, the
whole station's Billingsgate blue!'

Roger forced a laugh, but he was very thoughtful on
the way to see Maisie.

Chapter Ten

CELL

The strange thing was that the woman looked more attractive against the pale grey of the cell walls. As the policeman in charge of cells opened the barred door, she stood up from the narrow bed where she had been sitting reading, and tossed the book aside. She wore a loose-fitting linen shirt-blouse, she hadn't made-up so much, her hair seemed dressed closer to her head. Roger stepped inside and a detective sergeant stood just outside when the door was locked again.

'Well, Maisie,' Roger said. 'I hope you feel more like talking.'

She spoke in a controlled voice which made the words sound even more vicious than they were.

'You crummy bastard, what makes you think I'll ever talk to a cop?'

Roger studied her closely, but didn't speak immediately.

'Lost your tongue?' she sneered. She raised both hands, the nails overlong and clawlike, and made a gesture of dragging them down his cheeks. '*That* shows how gutless you are. You bloody nearly jumped out of your skin. Come on, tell me! What makes you think I'll ever talk to a cop?'

Roger answered evenly, 'Two things, Maisie.'

'Who gave you the right to call me Maisie,' she demanded.

'Two things,' repeated Roger equably, ignoring her

last question. 'First if you tell the truth now, then we
won't have to hold you on a charge of perjury; as things
are you could have that hanging over your head for
months. Second, if you tell the truth now, we could do
something about the charge of wilfully obstructing a
policeman in the course of his duty.'

'That would let you off the hook,' Maisie sneered. 'And
believe me you're well and truly on it. Handsome West
tries to rape innocent girl—can't you see the headlines?'

Roger laughed.

'What I'm looking for is the innocent girl!'

'Why you—' she began, and then she drew back, the
expression on her face changed, and she gave a reluctant
laugh. 'Do you know, if you weren't a cop, I could like
you.'

'Ah!' said Roger quickly. 'Then we do have some kind of
rapport. And I could like you well enough to believe you'd
tell the truth because you think it's the right thing to do.'

Now, her face resumed its original sneer.

'Don't make me laugh!'

'Maisie,' Roger said. 'You can save me and the police a
lot of trouble. You can save other witnesses a lot of
trouble. And at the same time you can save *yourself* a lot
of trouble, simply by telling me who bribed you to lie in
the witness box.'

She caught her breath.

'I didn't lie!'

'Of course you lied,' insisted Roger. 'And your friends
will lie too, if they're put in the witness box, but even-
tually we'll find out.' He moved his position a little and
her gaze swivelled round, she was so intent on him. 'Rapelli
wasn't with you during the hours you say he was. And if
you or anyone else, including your friend Fogarty, think
that by killing police witnesses who can prove Rapelli was
somewhere else you will keep the truth from coming out,

you're wrong.'

Maisie's eyes narrowed.

'No one killed anyone,' she retorted.

'Rapelli killed Verdi.'

'Crap!'

'And Fogarty killed one of the men who saw what happened at the Doon Club,' Roger added with great deliberation.

'*Fogarty* wouldn't kill—'

'He ran a man down on a zebra crossing. I told you so.'

'Oh,' she said, as if with relief. 'He was drunk.'

'There was no alcohol content in his blood.'

'None in Fogarty's? That's a laugh!' But despite her words, Maisie began to look worried. 'Did you catch him last night?'

'Yes.'

'So that's why he didn't come back,' she said, with a sigh. Then her lips set in a faint smile, and she went on, 'So I've heard what you wanted to say and it doesn't amount to a row of beans.'

'Maisie,' said Roger in a quiet voice, 'did Rachel Warrender know you'd been bribed to say Rapelli was with you the night before last?'

For the first time, he really pierced her guard. She faced him squarely, her eyes still narrowed, her hands clenched in front of her breasts. He heard the depth of her breathing, sensed that she was fighting an inward battle with herself, wondered if she would talk. Then her lips curled, and he knew that for the time being, at least, he had failed.

'You crummy copper,' she answered. 'Rachel Warrender wouldn't know a thing which wasn't straight up and down, crosswise and diagonal. She couldn't have known what wasn't true, anyhow.'

She turned away, flounced on the bed showing a lot of leg, and picked up the book. He saw, with a surprise which even broke through his disappointment, that it was Huxley's *Brave New World*.

* * *

Fogarty, who had been brought to this police station, swore that he could remember nothing of the accident the previous night.

Hamish Campbell simply refused to answer questions; refused even to admit that he had deliberately side-tracked the policeman who had been watching him before he had reneged as a police witness.

The smaller man who had been outside Fogarty's room with Campbell was named Pearson, Walter Pearson, a freelance photographer.

'Campbell told me he had a juicy picture for me,' he said. 'So I brought my camera. That's all I know, Mr. West. I swear that's all. I didn't have anything to do with what happened, I swear I didn't.'

Roger thought he was probably telling the truth, but he said, 'We'll see what the magistrate says.'

'Oh God, don't put me in court,' Pearson cried. 'My wife will knock the hell out of me if you do.'

Roger found it difficult not to be sorry for him.

He left the calls and went upstairs, then straight to the Yard and up to his office, mulling over all that had been said, particularly over Maisie's surprising reaction to the question about Rachel Warrender. So far Fogarty hadn't been charged, and it might be advisable to let him go and have him followed.

When he reached the office, more reports were in. Pearson was what he claimed to be, and his wife had been on the telephone twice, demanding his release. West put that report, from Information, aside, and read another. For the first time he learned that Hamish Campbell had a room in the same house as Fogarty.

Well, well.

'I wonder who else lives there,' Roger mused aloud, and sending for Danizon, he told him to have all the tenants checked. After telephoning Fulham to have Fogarty charged with driving a car with intent to cause grievous bodily harm, and Pearson with loitering, he then settled down to decide what to do next. There was one noticeable fact about the three prisoners: none of them had demanded to see a lawyer. Why not? Did they believe that they would be represented and well-looked after—by Rachel Warrender, for instance?

It was now after six o'clock; Roger flicked a thought towards Janet and Scoop, then lifted a telephone.

'Get me Miss Rachel Warrender of Warrender, Clansel and Warrender, solicitors—Lincoln's Inn,' he added.

'Very good, sir,' said the operator.

Would the girl be in? Roger wondered. Girl? How old was she?—twenty-three or four, he had thought, but Artemeus was sure she was older. He could recall her face vividly, the sharp features and the arched lips, the imperious brown eyes. He waited for the call to come through, concentrating on her, on Maisie's outburst, then on Benjamin Artemeus. Suddenly he pressed the bell for Danizon, who came in promptly. He was obviously not planning to go anywhere tonight, thought Roger.

'Yes, sir?'

'Artemeus, Benjamin,' Roger said.

'Yes?'

'Where did you call him?'

'At the Savoy Grill, sir. I left a message.'

'Did he call you from his office, do you know?'

Danizon frowned. He had a rather round, plump, earnest face, and would, Roger frequently thought, need little make-up to look like a circus clown.

'He spoke direct to me, sir. No secretary came on the

line first.'

'Check if he came on direct to the operator,' Roger ordered. 'In fact check Allsafe for details about him on Monday, and let me have a report as soon as you can.'

'Right, sir!'

'You off, now?'

'I'll be here for another hour at least, sir. I'm getting my files bang up to date.'

'That's good.' Rogger nodded dismissal, and as Danizon went out the telephone bell rang. Was it Rachel Warrender or was he too late for her?

'West here,' he said briskly.

'Your call to Miss Warrender,' the operator told him, and after a brief pause she added, 'You're through.'

Roger said quietly and pleasantly, 'Hallo, Miss Warrender. This is Superintendent West. I'm glad I caught you before you left the office.'

'I am usually here until seven,' Rachel Warrender replied in a studiously calm voice. 'How can I help you?'

'I thought I might be able to give you a little information,' Roger stated.

'If you are going to attempt to justify your arrest of Maisie Dunster, you are wasting your time,' Rachel retorted, coldly.

'That wasn't exactly the point,' Roger assured her. 'I'll justify that in the court whenever I have to. Did you know she was arrested in the room—in the *bed*—of a man who ran down and killed one of my witnesses against Rapelli?'

'Nonsense!' exclaimed Rachel.

'We'll prove how true that is on Monday, too,' Roger said. 'And I can tell you that I have reason to believe that my other witnesses have been under pressure to withdraw their evidence. Moreover I believe Maisie Dunster was paid to give false evidence. Don't you think you have gone too far?'

There was a long pause. He wished he could see her face and the expression in her eyes, but he could not even imagine how she looked. But he did not have to imagine the lift in her voice, her obvious and deep satisfaction, when at last she spoke.

'So you haven't a reliable witness left against Mario?' she remarked.

Roger said rather weakly, 'Haven't I?'

'You can't have! One is dead and the other terrified of being caught out in a lie.'

'Miss Warrender,' Roger said. 'I strongly advise you to discuss this case with one of your senior partners before you jump to any further conclusions. I really do.'

'How very chivalrous of you,' said Rachel, the lilt still in her voice. 'Goodnight.' He thought she was on the point of putting the receiver down when she spoke again, quickly, almost eagerly. 'Shall I see you in court on Monday? Or will you think better of it this time, and stay away?'

Lightly, Roger retorted, 'I thought we might go together.'

He rang off, nothing like as pleased with the remark as he sounded. It had been trite, and the young woman had had the best of the telephone encounter; she was still very sure of herself. He was as nearly sure as he could be that she felt secure in whatever she was doing, or else had no idea of what was going on. She might be much more worried than she pretended, of course, and putting up an act, but she was very sharp-witted and probably as sure of herself as she sounded. Thoughtfully, almost ruefully, he sat back in his chair. It was twenty-five minutes to seven, and nothing on his desk was desperately urgent. He could go home for dinner and come out again for another questioning session with the three prisoners if he thought it worthwhile.

Then he snapped his fingers and snatched up the receiver, called the police station where prisoners needed close to the Yard were held, and said, 'Suprintendent in charge, please.' Almost at once a man with a pronounced Lancashire voice spoke.

'Superintendent speaking.'

'Sam,' said Roger, knowing that this was an old stager, Superintendent Sam Otley. 'You've a man named Pearson under charge of uttering threats and common assault—'

Otley broke in with a guffaw.

'Poor devil! Have you seen his wife?'

'No. What's she like?'

'Two-Ton Tessie to the life except for Tessie's sweet temperament,' said Otley. 'She's huge—God knows what they look like together in bed. He's a shrimp, she—'

'Sam,' interjected Roger, warningly.

'Eh? Oh! Well, she's been round here at least three times. Once she threatened to throw the duty sergeant down the steps! Wouldn't be surprised if she couldn't do it, too. You can hear her voice all over the station. What do you want with Pearson, anyhow?'

'Let him go,' Roger ordered.

'What?' screeched Otley. 'Once she gets him home she'll murder the poor creep. Give him a week's rest, Handsome. Ask for a remand in custody on Monday; after a week she'll have cooled down a bit.'

'Let him go at half past seven,' Roger insisted.

'But *why*?'

'I want him followed,' Roger said. 'He's a little too meek and mild and she's a lot too rumbustous for my liking. See where he goes and what happens.'

'Will you fix the watching?' asked Otley, his resistance ebbing.

'Yes,' Roger promised. 'Thanks, Sam.' He rang off and

then went into Danizon's room, saying as he opened the door, 'I want two men to go over to the Fulham station and to shadow Pearson when they let him out.'

'What's he done to deserve getting out?' asked Danizon.

'He's a good sprat to catch a mackerel,' Roger answered.

Danizon hesitated, then slapped his knee and laughed; and doing so, looked more clown-like than ever.

'And you want the mackerel!' he cried. Then he sobered. 'I'll fix it,' he added. 'Oh, before you go, sir, I've managed to get a quick line on the man Artemeus. He's fairly new on the board of Allsafe, been there two years or so, I gather. He was with one of the big banks for several years as Chief Security Officer, and then Allsafe—'

Danizon stopped abruptly, as an idea suddenly struck him, his expression one of utter consternation.

'Good Lord, you're—you're *not* going to join them, sir, are you?' he asked. When Roger didn't answer, he went on in tones of even greater distress, 'You *can't*, sir. It would be a disaster!'

'Tom,' said Roger at last, lying not only to soothe this man but also to make as sure as he could that no rumours circulated round the Yard that night or in the next few days; it was often said, and only half in jest, that after the House of Commons Scotland Yard was the biggest talking shop in town. 'We are finding out whether some of the work we do overlaps with the security firms wastefully. Better not spread it around, though, or a lot of other people could jump to the wrong conclusion.' Then he chuckled. 'But I'm not as important as all that, Tom.'

'Don't you believe it,' rejoined Tom Danizon, and there was no shadow of doubt that he spoke from the heart. 'This place would damn near collapse without you. What you don't understand, if I may say so, is that the whole Yard's behind you.'

'In what?' asked Roger, startled.

Tom Danizon winked broadly.

'I know you can't admit anything or say anything about it, sir, but everyone knows about your little brush with the great white chief yesterday. And they hate his—I mean, they don't really appreciate a man who comes in from one of the other services and starts laying down the law to us. A question of teaching your grandmother how to suck eggs, really. Anyhow, sir, the whole of the C.I.D. staff and a lot from the other departments are right behind you. And it's bloody well time someone here had the guts to start leading with their right—like you did in court yesterday. And it's time we coppers were allowed to do our job instead of being hamstrung by a lot of half-witted regulations. Supposing you *did* go into the room on your own and found Maisie Dunster, by herself; no one in their right minds would think you'd lay a hand on her. Anyone who says different is a stinker, that's what I say.'

At last, Danizon stopped; and once stopped, fell into some confusion, as if embarrassed at having talked so freely. His talking had done one thing, however—enabled Roger to recover from his own surprise. And now he was ready with a question.

'Where did you get all this confidential information?'

Danizon looked even more embarrassed. Give him a pair of baggy trousers and he could walk straight into a circus, thought Roger irrelevantly, feeling a sudden warmth of affection for his assistant.

Danizon hesitated. 'Well, no names no pack drill, but we're behind you to a man. Do you know, there's even talk of a strike if you're suspended. Wouldn't surprise me if it came off, either. See what I mean when I say that we're with you?'

'Yes,' Roger said, very quietly. And he felt as touched and as humble as he sounded.

Danizon turned and fled.

Chapter Eleven

HOME

Roger drove along the Embankment towards Chelsea much more slowly than usual. It was already seven o'clock, and the West family ate at seven-thirty, whether he was home or not. It was a sunny evening with a light breeze, and the slanting sun made golden ripples of the muddy Thames. The south bank of the river seemed to sprout another big building every day, the skyline was forever changing. There was a wide stretch of road near the Albert Bridge, near his turn-off for Bell Street, and for the second night in succession he pulled into the kerb here.

It had really been a day.

The two most important things, in their way, had a delayed action effect. First, the offer from Artemeus, second the bombshell of Danizon's outburst. He had only been with Roger for a few months and although he had proved sound and reliable, Roger had never suspected him capable of such deep feeling. Not only was this surprising; there was also the astounding fact that what had happened in the commissioner's office had gone round the Yard so swiftly; who on earth had 'leaked' that information?

Coppell? he wondered hazily, then rejected the possibility. Coppell wouldn't stick his neck out so far. Then who? Roger couldn't even begin to imagine. He stopped trying, and passed to the other block buster: the

Yard's support for him, whether he was right or wrong. *He* hadn't even know that the story had spread, much less that the rest of the department had been lining up behind him.

Strike action!

'Oh, no!' he said aloud in a strangled voice.

A small foreign car pulled up behind him, and a moment later the door opened and a tall, dark-haired and—although Roger said it himself—good-looking young man uncoiled himself and came striding towards him. Roger opened the nearside door as Richard put his head in the doorway.

'Hi, Dad!' He had not only the deep, pleasing voice and broad, eager smile, but some elusive quality of like-ability, and Roger's heart rose.

'Hi, Fish!'

'Daydreaming?' asked Richard. 'Or working out all your problems? Hey, it's lovely out here. Give yourself a breather for five minutes.'

'Good idea,' said Roger, and he climbed out.'

He was a little taller and much broader than his son. They made a striking couple as they stood on the parapet, looking at gaily beflagged pleasure craft and a string of five barges, the first one pulling the others. Even the breeze was warm. Richard looked upstream, so that he could see Roger, who asked lightly, 'How have things been at the studio today?'

'Pretty lousy,' declared Richard. 'Not enough to do, that's my problem. Got a bit of luck, though. I'm going to Southern Ireland—Eire, you know—to make a film on Cromwell relics. Two other chaps are coming over and we'll be on a strict budget, but that's television all over. Pay a fortune for productions that aren't worth putting out, and mean as muck over films really worth making. I say, Dad.'

Richard broke off, eyeing his father intently, eagerly, a look which Roger had known since the boy had been six or seven. Roger knew perfectly well that some almost preposterous question was about to come forth with an earnestness to make it quite obvious that Richard was wholly serious.

'Yes?' asked Roger invitingly.

'Do you think there are such things as little people?'

Roger looked baffled, pondered—and then suddenly realised what his son meant: the elves and fairies which peopled the lore of most of Ireland and persisted in the minds of men.

'One of our technicians, a man named O'Hara, Paddy O'Hara, says that he's actually seen them,' Richard went on.

'Presumably at the bottom of his garden,' Roger said drily.

'Well, no, at the bottom of a well, actually, in his girl friend's garden.'

Roger gave a gust of laughter, while Richard surveyed him, his head on one side, completely detached from his father's mood and neither perturbed nor amused by the reaction.

'Fish,' Roger said. 'I don't believe there are such things as "little people".'

'Well, you could be right,' conceded Richard. 'And I suppose you could be wrong, too. It would be wonderful to be the first film unit to photograph them, wouldn't it! What a scoop! Er—' Richard's face changed its expression of gravity to one of tolerant concern. A year younger than his brother, he often behaved as if he were as old as his father. 'Talking about Scoop, what *about* Scoop? Had you expected anything of the kind? Like emigrating to Australia, I mean. It's a bit of a shock for poor old mum,' went on Richard, with glorious unconcern at the fact that he had asked a question and given Roger no chance to answer. 'She was pretty upset last night, wasn't she?'

'She could have been much worse,' Roger answered evasively.

'Poor old Pop! Never commit yourself to any side of family trouble.' Richard looked affectionately at his father for a moment, then went on, 'We'd better get a move on or she'll be after our blood for being late for dinner.' He looked at his watch and gave a whistle. 'Phew! Only five minutes. We must—' He hesitated, took a step towards his car, then turned to face Roger squarely, drew a deep breath, and asked, '*Is* it true you were nearly suspended today, Dad?'

Roger felt as if he had been struck, savagely, he was so taken aback. He actually backed a pace, without removing his gaze from Richard, who stood still, a little at a loss, but with a kind of doggedness about him. It wasn't simply that he behaved as if he were much older than his year; more that in a way he had caught up with his own maturity.

Roger let out a long, slow breath. Two couples, passing, looked at them curiously. A policeman came across the road, obviously because the two cars were parked on a clearway, but neither Richard nor Roger noticed him.

At last, Roger answered, 'Yes. How did you hear about that?'

'One of the chaps in our news room told me.'

'You mean it's going out on television?'

Suddenly, Richard looked young again; quite boyish.

'Oh, no, Dad! It's off the record. Mind you, it's all over televison headquarters, a lot of people have mentioned it. Say! there's one thing I've noticed, though. Generally they make a lot of cracks, had my leg pulled a hell of a lot this morning over that foul piece in the

Globe—everyone hates that rag, it's neo-nazi, that's what it is. But no one's made any cracks about this. All the remarks are: "Tell him to stick it out, Fish," and that kind of thing.' Now Richard's eyes were glowing. 'You've a hell of a lot of support among the Press and the jolly old public, Dad! Never knew how popular you were until today.' Then, suddenly, Richard's face clouded and a different tone deepened his voice. 'Say, Dad, you *haven't* been suspended, have you?'

Roger did not answer at once, he was too busy digesting what Richard had told him. Now he noticed the approaching policeman, but it was not until later that he realised that the man was within earshot.

'No, Fish, I haven't,' he said. 'But it was a close thing.'

*   *   *

'I heard it from his own lips,' Police Constable Ortega said over the telephone to his divisional headquarters. 'Handsome West himself. His son asked him if there was any truth in the rumour, and you should have seen Handsome's face. Like a graven image, it was. Then he said in the hardest voice *I've* ever heard, "No, Richard," he said, "I have *not*." Then he paused and you should have seen the look on his face. "No, my son," he said, "I have not, but it was a very close thing."'

*   *   *

'Hey, did you hear about Handsome West?' the divisional station sergeant said. 'The old basket nearly put him out on his ear.'

*   *   *

'I heard it from the sarge,' a divisional patrol-car driver

remarked. 'Handsome was practically suspended today. That old so-and-so, Trevillion. Who the hell do they think they are, at the Home Office these days? Lot of dictators. We want a man who knows the Force at the head, not a bloody dictator from the Navy or anyone else.'

*　　*　　*

'What's that?' said a man who caught some of this conversation over the radio telephone. '*West* suspended? That'll cause it!'

*　　*　　*

'West suspended. West out on his neck. West forced to resign. West told the commissioner where to get off.'
So the story sped on wings of rumour, from the Yard and divisions out to the sub-divisions and the men on the beat with their walkie-talkies, to the policemen in the ordinary cars and the Flying Squad cars. It spread from policemen everywhere in London to the county police whose areas adjoined the huge sprawl of the Metropolitan Police area, and then to all the county and regional forces. It spread to the railways, the airports, the Port of London Authority Police, and it was picked up by crews of aircraft flying from Heathrow to the ends of the earth.
'West's out, West's out, West's out!'

*　　*　　*

Three times in the course of that evening, Benjamin Artemeus was telephoned in his luxurious penthouse flat, each time to be told the same rumour. At ten o'clock he telephoned Lord Dean, Chairman of the Allsafe Board, passed on the rumours, and said confidently, 'It's only talk, so far, but it will become stronger and stronger.' He laughed. 'I'll see to that! And if he's not out on his neck already, he will be very soon. So we'll have him with us.'

'It's important—very important—that we do,' said Dean.

'Don't I know it,' replied Artemeus, and laughed again.

*　　*　　*

Roger put his car in the garage, Richard parked his outside the house, and they walked together along the crazy-paving path towards the back garden and the rear entrance. Every neighbour seemed to be out in the flower-decked gardens. Lawn mowers were turning, shears snapping, spades were going 'suck' into the hosed and soggy soil, hoes were scraping, women were bending over flower borders, taking off the heads of tulips and the blooms of wallflowers which had been spoiled by the rain of the past few days. The blue forget-me-nots had lasted well, the flowers tiny, yet larger than usual.

'Dad,' Richard said, suddenly close to the back door.

'Yes?'

'Are you going to tell mum about the suspension talk?'

'I don't think so,' said Roger. 'I think she has enough on her hands with Scoop at the moment.'

'Okay,' said Richard, and his eyes lit up. 'Mum's the word for mum!' He strode ahead of his father and into the house, calling, 'Hallo, Mum—the pride of the family's home. Moth-er! Where are you?'

Roger was in the doorway in time to see Janet appear at the passage door looking at her most attractive. She was smiling, apparently not weighed down by the prospect of Martin's coming emigration. Richard gave her a hug, exerting mock strength, and then held her at arm's length.

'Where's my dinner? I break my neck trying to get home

for little mother's daily dinner deadline, and what do I
find? Mother—dolled up in her best. No apron, no floury
hands, no dinner.'

'Idiot,' Janet said, obviously revelling in this. 'Ten
minutes.'

'But I'm hungry *now*!'

'You stay hungry for ten minutes,' Janet ordered, and
Richard allowed himself to be pushed aside. 'Hallo,
darling,' she said to Roger. 'I'm sorry I'm late but I've
been going through Scoop's clothes, we'll simply have to
buy him some new ones, we can't have him going round
Australia like a tramp.'

'But that's exactly what he'll be,' put in Richard.

'Oh go and telephone Lindy or find some other way to
fill in your time.' Janet pushed her son towards the door,
Roger touched her shoulders and gave her a light kiss on
the cheek. 'It will be nearer twenty minutes,' she amended,
and then looked intently into Roger's eyes. 'You haven't
got to go out again, have you?'

'I may have to, later,' Roger answered, 'but I've at least
a couple of hours.'

'That's something,' Janet said in an artificial voice
betraying a bitter word. 'Why don't you take the papers
and have a drink in the sitting room while I'm finishing
off?'

Roger washed, slipped on an old jacket and worn
leather slippers, had his drink, and went into dinner.
Scoop arrived late, obviously pleased with life; and the
boys kidded a great deal. They cleared the table between
them, then Richard went up to his room to do some work
on his Irish trip and Martin up to a box-room where he
painted. Roger went into the kitchen and dried up as
Janet washed. She was preoccupied, presumably about
Martin, so they said very little. Roger allowed his thoughts
to roam, from Richard and his startling question, to the

case, to Artemeus's offer, and to the simple fact that he couldn't make up his mind whether to tell Janet about that or not. If he told her, she would almost certainly want him to leave the Yard, and he would readily understand why. Her anxious 'You haven't got to go out again, have you?' was a vivid reminder of her constant complaint. They could never plan to go anywhere or do anything together with any certainty, he was so often called out. A job which paid a fortune and which would leave him free at weekends would be a dream to her.

She had often been edgy over the past few months, and if that was hardly surprising of a woman in the late forties, it wasn't the easiest situation to live with, especially in a household of men. Scoop's doubts about telling her directly, Richard's only half-pretended apprehension about being late for dinner, his own doubts about telling her of the Allsafe offer, were all indicative of the home problems. They weren't acute but one could never be sure when there would be some kind of emotional upheaval. And so far they had escaped lightly over Scoop's plans.

He put the last of the china on the kitchen dresser, she wiped the last burnished saucepan and hung it from a head-height shelf. Then she turned and asked with sharp intentness, reminiscent of one of her edgy moods. 'What is it that has to be so "mum" with mum? What were you talking to Richard about? What can you discuss with him and not with me?'

Chapter Twelve

CLASH

Roger looked into her face, and felt a sudden surge of love for her. At times such as when Richard had been fooling with her, she looked exactly like the girl she had been when they had met and married. Now, she was tense and anxious. She was, of course, bound to suffer some delayed action from the shock of last night's news; whatever else, he thought protectively, he must soothe and help her.

So, he laughed.

'You think it's funny,' she exclaimed.

'I think it's very funny,' Roger said.

'Well, I don't think it's funny at all.' Her eyes were over-bright, and they sparked with anger which must have been brewing all the evening. 'Are you going to tell me what it is? Or are you going to hold a family conference to decide whether I can be trusted with the information?'

Roger suddenly felt very tired. He'd hoped to keep it from her—hadn't wanted to worry her with this particular problem—but he'd have to tell her about it now, of course. He slipped an arm round her shoulders.

'There's a rumour in Fleet Street, one that reached Richard's studio, that I have been or am about to be suspended by the commissioner,' he explained. 'I went to a room expecting to find a man and instead found a woman. The situation was somewhat compromising.

Richard heard something about this at his studio, otherwise I wouldn't have said a word to him.'

As he talked, her expression changed from anger to anxiety, then to alarm. She didn't relax, didn't speak immediately, and Roger made himself go on, 'The whole thing might blow over in a day or two and be forgotten, so I didn't think there was any point in worrying you about it. Where were you when you heard what Richard said?' he added, in an attempt to take the tension out of the situation.

'In the bathroom.' That was immediately above the path at the side of the house. 'Why have you been in disgrace?'

Roger tightened his lips, but fought back a sharp retort, saying, 'I don't think "disgrace" is the right word. The commissioner disapproves of—'

'You making wild accusations in court, and going into a prostitute's room alone when *she's* alone. I have friends in Fleet Street, too, and one of them telephoned me to find out if I know. How often do such situations arise in the course of duty?' Now Janet was really at her emotional worst, her hands clenching and unclenching at her sides. 'The commissioner would hardly make such a fuss if this were an isolated instance, would he?'

Again, Roger spoke very slowly.

'Jan, I don't think now is the time to discuss this.'

'Well, I do!'

'Oh,' said Roger. 'You do.' Whatever happened, he thought, he must not lose his temper. He must see the funny side of the situation, must be understanding of the tensions which were tearing at his wife. He tightened his arm about her shoulders, feeling them stiff and unyielding. 'Jan,' he said, 'had the commissioner known what really happened there wouldn't have been any fuss. Coppell knew the whole story, and he calmed the old man down. I didn't know the girl was in the room, and when I heard her breathing I was going to get out but a couple of men had other ideas, pushed me back in, and slammed the door. Then the woman pulled a gun on me. It was really very simple and very silly, and I don't really know why the old man made an issue of it.'

'Well,' Janet said, in a strangled voice, '*I* know.'

'Do you, then!'

'And don't be flippant, Good gracious, don't you know me well enough to realise that when I'm worked up like this I don't want to be teased? He made an issue of it because you're *always* breaking the regulations. You just can't accept discipline, and *he* knows you can't have an efficient Police Force without discipline. Why on earth you can't be like other men and just do your job without volunteering for duty and every dangerous case there is, I shall never know. You're *always* working. Do you know we haven't had an undisturbed evening together for over two weeks?' When Roger didn't respond, and there was really no way he could, for she was undoubtedly quite right about that she went on, 'Well, I hope you *are* suspended.'

'Jan, please—'

'I hope you're suspended and I hope you're fired, or have to resign. *Then* perhaps you'll be able to lead a normal home life and your over-developed sense of duty can be devoted to your family, and not wasted on a lot of criminals who ought to be horsewhipped. You don't work for the police, you slave for them!'

Roger took his arm away, and moved to the open doorway. He hadn't seen her in such a mood for a long time, six months or more, and he kept reminding himself that this was the delayed action after hearing about Scoop's decision. It might not be reasonable, but somehow he had to ride it, had to help her to recover.

'Well,' he said, 'I won't slave for them forever.'

He could almost *see* Benjamin Artemeus over her shoulder; and he did see the sudden change in her expression, the hopeful gleam in her eyes, the new intentness. It was as if she divined that he had some outstanding news for her. And now he had to decide whether to tell her about the Allsafe offer. Swift as light, thoughts flashed through his mind; and finally, decision.

In such a mood as this, he couldn't possibly tell her; she wouldn't rest until she had persuaded him to say 'yes', and he was a long, long way from feeling sure that he wanted to leave the Yard. He needed days, probably weeks, to study all the implications both of staying and leaving.

'What do you mean?' she demanded. '*Are* you going to retire?' Her eyes blazed with new hope and she took him by the shoulders and talked as she would sometimes to the boys. 'Roger! Promise me you'll retire soon. *Soon*. If you want to make me happy again you'll have to leave the Force, especially now that Martin is going off. I shall be on my own so much in the evenings. When Martin's home it's not too bad, even if he's upstairs painting I can go up and have a chat with him if I'm at the end of my tether. But with him gone and Richard likely to get married at any time, I shall go mad here on my own in the evenings. Roger, you've got to retire. Do you hear? You've got to.'

And suddenly, her intensity being so great, she began to shake him. And she was still shaking him when the telephone bell rang and kept on ringing.

*   *   *

Roger had to answer the telephone.

Janet was shaking him so furiously, oblivious of everything, that he had to get away, had to have time to recover from the onslaught. The telephone went on ringing, and wrenching himself free, he said brusquely, 'I must answer that.' Going to the door of the passage, he saw Scoop standing by the telephone, and knew at once, by the set of his chin, the hurt but wary expression in his eyes, that his son had overheard at least the last things Janet had said. Gripping his son by the forearm, surprised, as always, at the boy's muscular strength, Roger picked up the telephone at the same time.

'This is Superintendent West.'

'Hi, Handsome,' a man said. 'This is Bobby Nixon.'

'Hallo, Bob,' Roger made himself say. Usually he could divorce himself from the home situation, no matter how tense, and apply himself to the problem coming from the Yard, but tonight it was much more difficult than usual. Nixon was a divisional superintendent who often acted as a stand-in for divisional men on leave, and Roger wasn't sure whether he was stationed at the Yard or not at the moment. 'Where are you?'

'Fulham.'

'Oh.'

'I've just been to see a girl friend of yours,' went on Nixon with heavy humour. 'Maisie Dunster.'

'How is her language?' enquired Roger.

'Meteoric—or rather, a bit like the aurora borealis. She wants to see you.'

'Then perhaps she'd better wait.'

'I should come over,' advised Nixon. 'I think she's in a very chastened mood, as a matter of fact. She's just had a visit from her lawyer, that Warrender girl.' Roger caught his breath at that piece of information. 'I don't know what happened, I wasn't there myself, but the turn-key said that after about five minutes they had a flaming row. Rachel Warrender left her, and Maisie bellowed a

few choice obscenities after her. Or do I mean blas-
phemies? I saw the Warrender girl out myself, and she
looked like murder.'

Roger asked sharply, 'When was this?'

Now, he was exclusively concerned only with work; the
conflict with Janet had faded into the background; so
had Scoop. He released the lad's arm, pointed upstairs
and then put a finger to his lips, wanting to tell Scoop
not to let his mother know what he had overheard and
then he concentrated absolutely on what Nixon said.

'Half an hour ago,' Nixon answered. 'Maisie went on
the rampage for a bit, threw everything she could lay her
hands on about the cell, then she calmed down and asked
to see me. So I went down, and she said she wanted to talk
to the great West. I should certainly come if you possibly
can, Handsome.'

'I'll be there in half an hour,' Roger promised, and
rang off.

He did not even begin to guess what had happened
between Maisie Dunster and Rachel Warrender, but he
knew Nixon was right; it was of the utmost importance
that he went to see Maisie while she was in her present
mood. And it could be a good thing, too—forcing a
break from Janet, who would almost certainly become
contrite and remorseful in a little while. But he had to
decide how to guide Martin.

Martin whispered, 'All right, Dad. I won't let mum
know that I heard.' He gave his father's arm a squeeze,
in turn, and then went back upstairs, remarkably agile
for such a heavy youth.

Roger went back into the kitchen.

There, Janet was sitting in the armchair, one hand at
her forehead; obviously crying. She looked up as he
approached, tears spilling down her cheeks.

'I'm—I'm sorry,' she said, huskily.

'Forget it, Jan.' Roger put his arm about her shoulders again, and squeezed. 'I know what a strain it is. Forget it.'

'I—I hate myself.'

'Well, I don't hate you,' Roger said mildly. 'I hope that counts for something. Love, I have to go out, but I don't expect to be long. Both the boys are home tonight. Shall I see if one of them can come down?'

'Oh, not yet!' Janet was alarmed, and began to run her fingers through her hair. 'I don't want them to see me like this. I've some ironing to do, and some sewing. I'll be all right for an hour. Provided there's someone in I'm always all right,' she added, forcing a smile. 'You go on, dear.'

Roger kissed her damp cheek, and went out.

As he walked into the cool of the evening, he felt numbed. It was a little after half past nine, quite early, but already it had been a long day. What time had he started? About six o'clock, or rather earlier. And he had been running into different situations ever since, all of them unexpected and each needing much more concentration than he had yet been able to give it. As he got out of the car, he thought that in a way this last had been the worst situation, for it had crashed upon him at home, where he should reasonably expect and where he most certainly needed relaxation. There was a cold spear of apprehension within him. If Janet were going to react like this after Martin had gone, what would life be like? He, Roger, couldn't take too many such scenes, and they had been going on periodically, for a long time.

Gradually, that gloomy apprehension faded and he began to think of Maisie.

It was part of his tactics, born of experience, to go over everything he knew about a suspect before an interview. Thought of Janet faded again, Maisie took her place in his mind, and he went through a series of mental pictures from the first time he had set eyes on her in the witness box, to the time when he had seen her in the cell. There was no need to go and check the reports and his notes, he was quite sure that he recollected everything she had said and done.

At last, he reached the police station. Nixon was waiting for him, tall, lean man with a nearly bald head and large, rather prominent eyes—a sharp contrast to Coppell's, which were small and deepset.

'Didn't lose any time,' Nixon remarked as they shook hands. 'Always on the ball, that's my Handsome. Where are you going to interview her? Down in the cells? Or shall we bring her up here, and kid her along a bit? I daresay if she gets a glimpse of the outside world it will oil her tongue.'

'Upstairs is a good idea,' agreed Roger. 'Lay on some coffee, will you, and cigarettes? I'll go down and get her myself.'

'I'll send a man with you,' offered Nixon. 'With the caviar.'

Five minutes later, Roger saw Maisie, sitting with her legs up on the narrow bed, not putting on an act or posing. Her face was set more sombrely than he had seen it, obviously something had upset her very much. She nodded without speaking to Roger, looked surprised when she was taken upstairs, equally surprised to find coffee, cream and chocolate biscuits on a tray, and easy chairs to sit in comfort.

'Why the plush treatment?' she demanded. 'Think this will make me talk more?'

'It should make you feel more like a human being,' Roger retorted.

'And less like a louse,' retorted Maisie wryly. 'All right, Handsome—give me some of that coffee with a lot of milk and sugar, and I'll tell you the solemn truth, even if you send me to jail because of it.'

She looked sombre enough to suggest that she really believed that she was about to risk imprisonment.

The man whom Nixon had sent down had a notebook and pencil in his hands.

Chapter Thirteen

SEDUCTION

Maisie took a cigarette and thrust her face forward to get a light. Roger gave her time to drink half a cup of coffee, then squared himself in his chair.

'You know that anything you say may be taken down and used in evidence, don't you?' he said quietly.

'Yes,' she replied.

'Even with that, it's better to let us have the truth,' he went on. 'Did you lie about Rapelli being with you on Thursday night?'

'Yes,' she said.

'Were you paid to lie?'

'Yes.'

'How much did you get?'

'A hundred pounds,' she answered.

'Did you realise what a serious crime it was?'

She shrugged.

'One kind of lie is very much like another to me. What kind of sentence will I get?'

'If you go into the box next week and change your evidence, I doubt if you'll be charged. I'm not sure in the circumstances that what you said was permissible as evidence, anyhow.'

She looked astounded more than delighted, then, gradually, excitement sparked in her eyes. She stubbed out her cigarette and finished her coffee; Roger poured her another cup.

'But that's wonderful,' she exclaimed. 'Wonderful!'
Then a shadow passed over her face and she went on, 'The
trouble is, I may not have the hundred pounds to pay
back for—for saying what I did.'

'Whom will you have to repay?' asked Roger.

For the first time, she hesitated, and he wondered
whether she was in fact telling the truth, or whether this
could be a deliberate attempt at deceiving him. There
was absolutely no way of telling, and if she withdrew her
statement she would certainly be showing earnest of her
new-found honesty.

Then she said, 'Mario Rapelli.'

'He was driven to exclaim, *'Rapelli!'*

'Yes.'

'Did he also bribe the others?'

'Yes,' said Maisie. 'He paid us in advance, he said there
might be trouble.'

'Did he then!' exclaimed Roger. 'Then he knew in
advance—'

He broke off, biting his tongue, needing to think. If
Rapelli had gone to the club to kill Verdi, then the whole
situation changed, took on an even greater significance.

'How—ah—how long have you known him?' he asked.
He pictured the sallow, handsome face of the youth who
had been in the dock and remembered how impressed he
had been, how sorry he had felt for the boy.

'A few weeks,' said Maisie.

'How much did he pay in all?'

'A hundred for me and a hundred each for the others,'
Maisie answered.

'Did you know what the charge would be?'

'We knew we were to say he had been with us that
evening during those hours. Later when we heard what
he'd done, we thought it was a great joke at first. Mario

loves the guitar, and can't bear to get even a scratch on it—' She gave a hollow laugh. 'We didn't know it was going to be so serious,' she went on. 'Even *I* wouldn't have agreed if I'd known there would be a murder charge. Or anyhow,' she went on with a flash of honesty, 'I would have wanted at least five hundred pounds.'

'Why do you need the money?' Roger demanded.

'That's nothing to do with the police or anyone,' Maisie retorted, so tight-lipped that he was quite sure that it would be a waste of time forcing the question. 'I need a thousand, and I'm halfway there. That's all you have to know.'

'What about the hundred pounds from the photographer yesterday?' asked Roger.

'That would have been a big help,' she admitted. 'I'd have had only four hundred to go. You don't happen to know anyone who will give or lend me five hundred quid, do you?' She was half-joking, but her eyes betrayed the fact that she was half-serious, too.

'Can't Rachel Warrender help?' asked Roger.

There was no need for him to rub in the fact that earlier today she had talked so glowingly of Rachel, and this evening had had that violent quarrel with her. He saw Maisie frown, saw her lips tighten, and wondered whether he would get any kind of response.

At last, she said, 'No.'

'Why did you quarrel tonight?'

Maisie closed her eyes, and seemed to force each word out with an effort.

'I told her I'd lied,' she said.

'You told Rachel Warrender?'

'Yes.'

'So she thought you were telling the truth in court?'

Maisie looked resentful and it was a long time before she responded, still as if she were making a great effort.

'Yes. After the police charged him, Rapelli telephoned her and asked her to help him.' Maisie took another cigarette and it quivered between her lips as Roger held the flame for her, then went on huskily, 'She told him she wouldn't at first, but then she changed her mind and came over to my place and questioned all of us. She hadn't the slightest idea we were lying. We—er—told her all four of us were having fun and games in bed, and she was pretty disgusted, but she was certainly fooled.'

'I see,' said Roger. 'Well, it was quite an alibi, even if it was phoney. Tell me, *do* you ever disport yourselves four to a bed?'

She threw back her head and laughed with surprising heartiness as she replied, 'It has been known! We have to be hopped up, and once we are, then inhibitions go out of the window, orgies come in at the door! I think you have to be a pretty wild person, wild in sexual life, I mean, to start it, but once you do—' She broke off, letting smoke drift up past her face and considering him through it; it gave a touch of mystery and of greater sophistication to her expression. 'Handsome,' she went on, still with a hint of laughter in her voice, *'you're* shocked, aren't you?'

Roger pursed his lips.

'You are,' she insisted. 'I can sense it. My, my, what innocents our policemen are! No wonder so many criminals can get away with murder.' She laughed again. 'We're really quite mild, you should visit some of the Soho and Chelsea orgy-parties!'

'We do,' said Roger drily. 'When we raid them. So Rapelli was so anxious to escape from the charge that he paid out two hundred pounds for you all to lie for him. How well do you know him?'

'I've had a night or two out with him,' Maisie answered. 'You have to admit he's a handsome type, and although he may not look it, I can tell you he's quite a man!'

'Oh, I admit it!' said Roger. 'So he paid you and the others in advance to lie, and you told Rachel you were telling the truth, she believed you and thought, with your evidence, she could get Rapelli off. Thanks, Maisie. I'll have a little talk with him soon. Where does Fogarty come in on this?'

'Fogarty is quite a man, too,' she stated.

'And you,' said Roger, 'are quite a woman.'

'That's right,' said Maisie. 'Sexual or multi-sexual or whatever the psychoanalysts call it. Did you see *The Man From La Mancha*?' When Roger nodded, she threw back her head, and, to Roger's astonishment, burst into one of the songs from the show. She had a full, ringing voice and the acoustics of the cell block suited it perfectly.

> *'One pair of arms is like another,*
> *'I don't know why, or who's to blame.*
> *'I'll go with you or with your brother.*
> *'It's all the same.'*

Then she stood up and with a lift of head and surge of bosom she reached a crescendo with a purity of note which made the man with them drop his ballpoint pen, brought two policemen to the foot of the cell steps and several other prisoners to the bars of their cages to hear although they could not see.

> *'They're all the same ...'*

The notes echoed and re-echoed so loudly that it almost seemed as if she were still singing. Then she dropped her hands and covered her eyes with one hand, groping for her chair with the other. The last echoes faded.

'That's me,' she said, hoarsely.

'Maisie,' asked Roger, 'do you go from man to man just to make money?'

'That's right,' she admitted.

'Won't you tell me why you want the thousand pounds?' he almost pleaded.

'No, I will not.'

'All right.' Roger stood up. 'Would you rather stay here for the weekend or would you rather go home?'

He so startled her that she stood back a pace, staring at him, her eyes widening, and for a few moments there was absolute silence in the room. Then, in a taut voice, she asked, 'Would you really let me go?'

'Yes. I made the charges and I should proceed with them, but if you undertake to appear in court on Monday morning, you can go home tonight.' When she didn't answer, he went on, 'You don't have to. I'm giving you a choice.'

In a mumbling voice, she answered at last, 'I'd like to go home.'

'Right,' said Roger briskly. 'As I live in Chelsea I'll run you there on my way.' He stood up. 'We'd better have a word with the superintendent before we leave.'

Nixon, far too experienced a policeman to show any surprise, went through the formalities of release, and, at Roger's suggestion, promised to send a patrol car after them.

'Don't want any more wild charges, do you?' he asked dryly.

Soon, they were on the way, Maisie next to Roger in front of his car, the police car a hundred yards behind. Maisie's thigh ran warmly against Roger's on the bench seat of his Morris and he did not know whether it was deliberate or not. She was staring straight ahead, not smoking; she had a pleasant profile; if she were not quite so plump she would be very pretty, he thought.

'Do you know Hamish Campbell?' he asked.

'No.'

'He was the man outside your door this morning.'

'I know—I saw the evening papers by the courtesy of the police! His name and photograph were there. I knew he was at the club where Rapelli hit Verdi over the head.'

'Do you know Pearson, the man who was with him?'

'No.'

'Did you know Verdi, himself?'

'No.'

'Did you know that Rapelli went to this Doon Club?'

'I knew he went to a lot of music clubs and discotheques, he was a nut on pop beat music and erotic dancing. There are a lot of nuts. Let me tell you this, Handsome, before you drop me—first right at the end here, then first left and the third house along,' she interpolated. 'Rapelli and I knew each other but we weren't in each other's pockets. I can tell you what he's like as a lover, but I don't know anything else about him—not that counts, anyhow.'

Roger made the two turns, and pulled up outside the house in which Maisie lived, one of several in a short terrace. This part of Chelsea was a strange mixture of architecture; there were a few Tudor cottages, at least one early Georgian house standing in its own grounds, and some early Victorian houses, all mixed with small blocks of modern apartments built on the sites of houses which had been bombed out of existence during the war.

Roger stopped, and leaned across her to open the door. She waited until he touched the handle, then, seizing his arm in a surprisingly tight grip, held it to her bosom. Leaning sideways and imprisoned as he was, his face a little lower than hers, Roger was acutely aware of her breath against his cheek. Maisie leaned forward, her eyes bright and mischievous, her lips parted. Suddenly she bent her head and thrust her lips against his, moving so swiftly that he had no opportunity to turn away. It was several seconds before she drew back, pushed open the car door, and thrust one leg out to the pavement.

'Handsome,' she said. 'I promised you the truth and now you know it all. I don't hate the way I earn my money. I have a very big appetite. I *eat* men. I could eat you. Come and see me when you're off duty. Just give me enough time to get nice and tarted up for you. Any time. And I don't mean as a paying guest, either. I mean just as a guest.'

She got out and slammed the door.

He sat without moving for what must have seemed a long time to the men in the patrol car. He wondered whether they could have seen anything through the rear window of his car, but their headlights had not been on and there was no street lamp near. It didn't much matter, anyhow. He flicked his lights and almost at once one of the men got out of the car and came hurrying towards him.

'Sir?' The man pushed his head close to the open window.

'I wasn't able to ask Mr. Nixon before,' Roger said, 'but I want you two to watch this house, particularly Miss Dunster, until some men come from the division to keep an eye on it and her. I'll talk to Mr. Nixon by radio.'

'Very good, sir.'

'Thanks. Goodnight.'

The man's 'goodnight' followed Roger as he began to move off. He drove slowly, turning the corner before calling Nixon and putting through the request which was tantamount to an order. Nixon made a light remark. 'Didn't think you'd let her go for the sake of it, Handsome. I'll fix it.' Roger grunted and rang off.

Now he had to make a quick decision.

He touched his lips, still slightly tender from the crushing pressure of Maisie's. He had never known a kiss like it, nor such a body, so demanding and yet so yielding.

It was lucky he was a staid old married man, he thought, smiling to himself and dismissing Maisie from his mind. There were three things he could do.

First, go back to Janet. She would be glad to see him, he felt certain, and anxious to make amends.

Second, go and question Rapelli. It was late and Rapelli, even if not asleep, would be tired and therefore more likely to talk. And if Rapelli once cracked, then the case was over.

Third, go and see Rachel Warrender, and chance her mood.

He knew that he should go back to Janet, that to force himself to go on working was an example of the excessive attention to duty which so often exasperated her. But if he went back and found that her mood had hardened, it would probably lead to an argument, possibly a near-quarrel which could carry them far into the night.

And he had to be fresh and fit next morning.

Chapter Fourteen

VISITOR

Roger yawned and rubbed his eyes. The truth was that he was in no shape to interview and interrogate anyone, wasn't alert enough and must not attempt it; there was no emergency, and he was nearer Bell Street than the Yard. So he would go home. As he drove slowly and with extreme care, he found his thoughts roaming at will over the past with Janet. In this part of Chelsea and along the embankment, across the river in Battersea Park and a little further afield, on Clapham Common, they had done most of their courting. He had been at the Chelsea division in those days and Janet had lived in the next borough: Fulham.

She had been so lively, pretty; damn it, beautiful!

As she was beautiful today. If only she would not get so upset!

Her time of life, of course, simply heightened moods which had always existed. In those courting days she had always been acutely disappointed and often angry when he had had to break a date. Several times he had nearly lost her. He gave a twisted smile at the recollection of that, and of jealousy. When a young man was in love as utterly as he had been there was a special kind of torment in being forced to leave one's beloved with others: knowing another man was playing tennis with her, or taking her home, or to the theatre or pictures.

And—his smile broadened—he remembered the first time he had been compelled to arrest a young woman who had resisted, almost savagely, and then turned all her considerable seductive charm on him, with Janet looking on.

Her voice came out of the past.

'You needn't have handled her like that... You actually seemed to enjoy it!' And for a while there had been tension, with his heart in his boots. It had been touch and go whether they had spent the rest of the evening together. But they had; that was the very evening when they had walked along Bell Street and, as a result, started their married life in the house where they still lived. There had been clashes, all of them—well, most—over the restrictions of his job. But all of these had passed, and if it were true that of recent years the conflicts had lasted for longer periods and tension sometimes dragged on, Janet would come out of the menopause and sooner or later he would retire.

The recollection that he could resign whenever he liked and take a job that would give Janet all she asked came out of the blue. He actually let the wheel wobble for a moment and forced a passing motorist to pull out. The driver glowered. Roger turned into Bell Street, and as he did so a man came out of one of the houses, turned towards King's Road and hurried away. There was something furtive in his manner, and Roger knew why.

The woman at that house, Natalie Tryon, was miserably unhappy, with a husband with whom she stayed only for her children's sake. This man was her lover, who visited her whenever her husband was away.

Roger pulled up outside his own house and turned towards the garage, then put on the brakes, appalled at a sudden, devastating thought.

Supposing *Janet* had a lover!

Supposing she had become so lonely and miserable that

she had sought and found consolation.

Wouldn't that explain her moodiness, her attitudes, her thinking?

Roger sat absolutely rigid, and had been there for three or four mintes, hardly able to think clearly, when a shaft of light appeared from the front door, and then Janet's silhouette appeared against the porch light.

'Darling! Is that you?'

He made himself call out, 'Yes, coming!' Opening the car door, he saw her hurrying towards him. The light from street lamps were soft on her face, and she looked at her best. She moved beautifully, too. Suddenly, she was close to him, and he closed the car door softly, habitually remembering not to wake a neighbour's baby. As suddenly, he took her in his arms, held her almost too tight for a moment, and then kissed her.

A few moments later, breathless, they drew apart. Neither spoke as they linked arms and turned towards the house, until Janet said, 'Will you leave the car out?'

'Yes, it doesn't matter on these warm nights.'

'I'll put it away if you like,' she offered.

'No. Leave it.' They reached the porch, still arm in arm. He knew that her mood had changed even more than his, that now she was calm in spirit. He did not know how to tell her what was passing through his mind, and she saved him the need to say anything.

'You lock up, I'll make some tea, darling, and we'll have it in the kitchen. The boys have both gone to bed. I'll pop up and get into a dressing-gown.'

'Good idea,' he said. He locked and bolted the front door, checked the windows of the sitting and dining rooms, then hesitated. He would be more comfortable in a dressing-gown, too, and especially in slippers. Quickly he went upstairs, and into their room.

He stopped short.

Spread across the bed were open photograph albums, loose snapshots and seaside pictures, and a glance showed that these were all of the days of their courtship and early marriage. None showed the boys, even as babies. The pillows were rucked up and the bedspread had been pulled down. On one pillow was a screwed-up handkerchief. Roger picked it up and found that it was damp; she had obviously been crying. He looked more closely at the albums; there they were at a tennis party, at a dance, with a crowd of young people on the beach: always together, always looking happy.

Roger lost himself in retrospection, now and again thinking: Thank God I came straight back tonight. He lost count of time, until, disturbed by a footfall on the landing, he looked up and saw Janet.

She came in.

'I meant to clear all that up before you came in here,' she said.

'Why, darling?'

She stood a little distance from him, and answered, 'It seemed like a kind of blackmail to leave them out!'

'Some blackmail! I've been think about those days, too. Remember that buxom blonde I arrested at the tennis club for raiding the dressing rooms?'

'Shall I ever forget her!'

'She wasn't unlike Maisie Dunster,' he told her. 'Only Maisie's much more attractive.'

'*And* seductive?' Janet, quite free from tension now, went on, 'Darling, I hate myself when I behave like I did tonight, I really do. No, don't interrupt.' She put a hand over his lips, and went on with words she had obviously rehearsed over and over again. 'I know you have the job to do, I know we've had this kind of upset before, I know there are times when I hate the job so much that I could climb on the roof and cry "down with Scotland

Yard!"—' She paused, momentarily, a gleam of laughter in her eyes. 'But deep down I also know that you love it more than I hate it, that you couldn't really live without the Yard but I can live with the situation even if I do have to let off steam sometimes. You needn't worry, you really needn't. Just—' She broke off again and went on with only a slight change of tone, 'Just keep me hopeful with promises of what we'll do when you do retire. After all, it won't be more than five years now, and we've had twenty-five already, so it isn't really too long.'

'No,' he said, huskily. And then, 'I'll keep you hopeful.'

'Don't promise you'll have every other weekend off and ten days' leave every quarter,' she protested, half-laughing. 'Just be with me as much as you can, darling. *Please*.' Slowly the laughter faded and there was a new earnestness, new intentness in her manner. 'You're all I've got, you know. The boys, bless them, aren't mine any longer, not in the true sense—and on a night like this they're on your side. I love you so much,' she went on quietly. 'Do you know, since those tennis club days I've never looked at another man. And—*darling!* Let me finish. I do *not* want to know whether you have looked at another woman. I really don't. I don't mind what you do provided you're happy, and I hate myself when I add to your problems.'

There were tears in her eyes.

And his eyes stung.

*   *   *

Later, when their bodies had intermingled with a passion which they had not known for a long time, they fell asleep.

When, just after half past seven, Martin brought in a tea tray, Roger was still holding her tightly.

'*Whoops!*' exclaimed Scoop. 'See you later.'

He put down the tray and fled.

*　　　*　　　*

On the Monday morning, Roger and Janet after waking early, were talking about the case. Relaxed in a chair by the bedside with Janet sitting against pillows, a bedjacket draped over her shoulders, Roger could see the whole series of incidents more clearly. Now and again Janet asked a question, for clarification, but for the most part it was a monologue. The tea was cold in the pot and the room warm from hot sunshine when the telephone bell rang. He picked up the extension by the side of the bed, and glanced at the clock. It was a little after nine.

'Roger West,' he announced, expecting someone from the Yard.

'Mr. West,' a woman said, and he knew at once that this was Rachel Warrender, 'I will be grateful if you can spare me an hour this morning.'

'I may not be able to fit in an hour,' Roger had to reply. 'Will half an hour do?'

'You're very kind. Shall I come to your office?'

'If you do, it will have to be official,' Roger said.

She hesitated for a moment, then said huskily, 'You're quite right, thank you. Where do you suggest?' Roger was looking at Janet and framing the name 'Rachel W' with his lips. Janet's eyes widened and she stretched out a hand, whispering, 'Roger!'

'Just a moment.' Roger covered the mouthpiece with his hand. 'Had a brainwave?'

'Why not ask her here?' Janet suggested. 'I could bring in some coffee or a drink, and I'd love to see her.'

It was a sensible idea, it would help to seal their new understanding, the new mood, and Roger turned back to the telephone.

'If you could be at my home in half an hour or so, we could talk here.'

'Oh, that would be splendid!' He had not heard Rachel Warrender speak with such spirit before. 'I may be a little more than half an hour, I'm at my office in Lincoln's Inn, but I'll be with you as soon as I can.'

She rang off.

As Roger replaced the receiver, Janet was getting out of bed. She edged towards the window, so that she couldn't be seen from the street. Stretching up to draw the curtains, her skin was so white, her figure so lovely, her hair so dark where it fell about her shoulders, that he caught his breath.

'If she'll be here in half an hour *I've* got to get a move on.' Out of the tail of her eye she saw him get up from the chair. 'Darling, you get shaved quickly. I'll have to make some toast—darling, you'll have to. I—*Roger!*' she almost screamed. 'Roger, there isn't time!'

'I know,' he said, enveloping her. 'And I'm nearly an old man.' He held her very tightly, then kissed her on the forehead and let her go. 'I'll get my own breakfast.'

He bathed, shaved, made toast, piled on butter and marmalade, made instant coffee, telephoned the Yard to say he would not be in the office until eleven thirty or so, checked that nothing new had developed over the Rapelli case and that Fogarty, Campbell and Rapelli, the only remaining three on any kind of charge, all appeared to have spent good nights. So far, so good.

'And Tom,' he said to Danizon, 'I must be in court when the charges against Campbell are made. Will you see that he's not heard until midday—noon—at the earliest?'

'Yes, sir,' Danizon said. 'What about Fogarty?'

'If he's released, make sure he's effectively trailed,' Roger said.

'I'll see to it, sir,' said Danizon. 'I can tell you that Mr. Coppell will be out most of the day, he's going to that conference of European Police. And the commissioner will be out too—he's going to the luncheon reception.'

Roger laughed.

'Almost a free day, in fact!'

'If I were you, sir,' said Danizon, 'I'd take at least part of the day off. Just go to court and—but I'm sorry, sir. I'm talking out of turn.'

Roger could almost see him go pink with confusion as he rang off.

A moment later, Janet came out of the sitting-room, a housecap sloping over one eye, a small apron over her nightdress. She carried a mop and a duster and a can of furniture-polish spray. Her nose and cheeks were shiny and her lips pale.

'I'll have my bath now and get dressed—you open the door when she comes. I'll bring coffee at a quarter past ten, is that right?'

'Ten o'clock,' urged Roger. 'I'm not sure how this inter-view will go, and I could make heavy weather of it.'

'Why?' asked Janet. 'Isn't she buxom enough for you?'

Five minutes later he was outside, snipping the fading heads off some scarlet parrot tulips and noticing the trimness of lawn and hedge which he had hardly seen during the pressures of the past few weeks. Did either of the boys help Janet much? he wondered. Or was this mostly her work? Practically nothing needed doing, he must remember to compliment her.

He was pulling a few weeds, mostly seedlings, when a car drew up. He looked through the thick privet hedge, able to see that it was a white M.G.: just the car he could imagine Rachel Warrender having. And it was her. She climbed out, and he was slightly startled by her appearance, for she wore a white linen trouser-suit, accentuating her youth and slimness of figure, and a small, round, sailor hat. Not at all the average person's conception of a woman solicitor, Roger thought amusedly. He felt sure that Janet, watching out of the window, would have eyes rounded in surprise.

'Good morning, Miss Warrender,' he called across the hedge. 'You found the house all right, then.'

She started, and turned to look at him. And now he was even more startled: in fact appalled. For she looked in terrible distress. Her beautiful eyes were shadowed, and so glassy that he doubted if she had slept all night. She nodded, and formed the words 'good morning', but did not utter a sound. He met her at the gate, and saw that there were tears in her eyes as well as lines at her forehead and mouth. He didn't shake hands but led the way to the front door, said, 'The door on the right,' and followed her into the sittingroom.

Roger doubted whether she would have noticed if this had been a pigsty, she was so preoccupied with her own problems. She sat down in a chair, looking so ill and troubled that he even found himself wondering whether she took drugs and was in urgent need of a shot.

Then, she looked at him very straightly, and said, 'Mr. West, I think you are the only man who can help me, and I'm not even sure that you will. May I tell you what is troubling me? And may I beg you to give me your advice?'

Chapter Fifteen

RACHEL

'If I can help, I certainly will,' Roger answered, gently. 'And if it's something which, as a policeman, I can't discuss, I'll tell you. Are you comfortable there?'

'Perfectly, thank you.'

'Will you have a cup of coffee, or—?'

'Nothing, thank you.' She sat upright, and placed her hands on the arms of her chair. 'In the beginning it was very simple, but I now believe that you were right and I was wrong. I am afraid that Mario Rapelli did attack Verdi. When I appeared in court I felt sure that he was a victim of conspiracy, and that the police wanted a conviction whether he was guilty or not guilty. I don't think that is true now.'

'I'm very glad,' Roger said; he wanted to hear all she had to say before asking questions.

'Even last night, when we talked, I hoped I was right first time. But I now have proof that Maisie lied in the witness box and that the other witnesses also lied to me. And I've made another discovery, Mr. West, in its way just as bad.' She leaned forward, her eyes seeming to grow bigger and bigger. 'I've had a private investigator checking. I know that the two men who saw the attack on Verdi, your two witnesses I believe, were approached and offered a substantial sum of money to renege. Smithson refused, but Campbell agreed.' Now, her face seemed nothing but eyes. 'Smithson is dead, and Campbell switched right round and tried to compromise you.'

When she stopped, Roger said evenly, 'Do you know who killed Smithson?'

'Fogarty, of course.' Rachel paused, as if to find the right word, then went on, 'I believe Fogarty was paid to run Smithson down. I know he claims to have been drunk but—did you know that he was practically a non-drinker?'

'The medical reports say that he had little or no alcohol in his blood that night,' said Roger.

'I should have known you would have discovered that,' remarked Rachel. 'My father—' She caught her breath. 'My father begged me not to take this case. Why was he so anxious I shouldn't take it? *Why*—?' She caught her breath again, and added, 'If the worst thing that happened as a result of this were a blow to my pride, it wouldn't matter a fig. But—'

Roger believed that she was coming to the crux of the visit. But there was a reservation in his mind, one he had to consider although emotionally he found the suspicion difficult to justify.

She could be fooling him.

These huge brown eyes which looked so weary could be affected by eye drops or by drugs. Her story could be partly false; she could be presenting the case in such a way as to disarm him, to convince him (and so the police) that if she had committed any crime it was unwittingly: that she was the victim of criminals who had used her as a front. Roger knew that any solicitor who knowingly represented an accused man who was bribing witnesses, would be struck off without mercy, and she must know this too. She could be fighting for her whole future in her profession.

He wanted to believe what she said, but so much

would depend on what she was going to say now.

Through tightly set lips, she went on, 'I don't think you know this, Mr. West, but Mario and I used—used to see a great deal of each other.' The words came as if she had to force each one out with a conscious effort. 'I—I loved him, Mr. West—but when I discovered he was meeting Maisie Dunster and going to all these odd parties, I stopped seeing him. Then, the other day, he telephoned me and said he was in trouble. It was such a shock, both what he told me *and* hearing from him again—I was just beginning to forget him—' Rachel bit her lip '—I told him I couldn't possibly take the case. Then, almost at the last minute, I changed my mind. That was why he looked so startled when I appeared in court. I believed what he'd told me, Mr. West—after all, it was because of Maisie and those—those *parties*, that I gave him up.' She laughed bitterly. 'But it now appears that he paid —bribed—all these people to lie for him. And bribed them *before* he attacked Verdi. If he'd struck Verdi in a fit of rage, I wouldn't have been so troubled. If he'd told me exactly what had happened, I'd have done everything humanly possible, I would have paid for the best possible counsel. But he deliberately lied to me. Deceived me. Found the money to pay these false witnesses. Yet he earns scarcely enough to keep himself; he has often borrowed from me.'

She paused, as if for breath, and now Roger no longer doubted her sincerity.

'Where is he getting the money?' Rachel asked chokingly. 'Who is financing him, and why? Did he attack Verdi for personal reasons, or was there some other reason? *Why* was my father so desperately anxious I shouldn't take this case? Can *you* find out, Mr. West? Before next Thursday when Mario comes up for the second hearing? I need to know before—before I decide whether to defend him or not. Can you, *please*?'

And now Roger thought he knew what she was asking.

She realised he would find out all he could about Rapelli and the murder, that he would go all out to get at the truth; and she wanted him to tell her, the defending solicitor, in advance. But he simply could not tell her except through the normal channels—and that would have to be at the trial. To help her before the police court hearing he would have to betray not only the general police code but his own standards.

Yet how could he say no?

*   *   *

Roger heard Janet come down the stairs, and guessed she would soon be in with the coffee. He wasn't at all sure that her presence would help this situation, but knew, after what had happened, that he could not keep her away. But he could prepare Rachel for her arrival and at the same time give himself the chance to think.

'Rachel,' he said, suddenly, 'my wife will bring some coffee in a few minutes. I would like to ponder this until she's gone.'

Rachel made no protest of any kind, and showed little reaction.

'You will consider it?' She sounded pleading.

'I will.'

'You—you're very good,' she said huskily.

Five minutes later Janet came in, looking fresh and elegant in a dark brown dress, her hair attractive, her make-up perfect. She was at her beautiful best, and carried off a situation like this as few others could. She was obviously curious but didn't ask questions; was pleasant and friendly but overdid nothing.

Suddenly, she stood up.

'Roger dear, do pour Miss Warrender some more coffee, when she's ready. I have to go out. Miss Warrender, I don't know whether to hope you win, or Roger, but I do hope you both come out of this case with credit.'

'Especially your husband,' Rachel said drily.

'If it has to be one or the other—yes!' Janet laughed, shook hands, and left. Rachel watched her go out of the room and then looked at Roger wonderingly.

'What a lovely woman!'

'We certainly agree about that,' Roger said, laughing. 'And I agree'—he sobered immediately—'that we have a difficult problem. I would like to help, but helping at this stage, if it were known, could create an intolerable situation for me. You have no idea what happens when a police officer stretches the law.'

'I can imagine,' Rachel said. She looked better, brighter, but there was tension in her voice again. 'Are you telling me nicely that you won't help?'

'No,' Roger said. 'I am simply saying that I need to study all the angles before I make you any promise. When must you know?'

'I don't need to know until Wednesday morning, I suppose,' she replied. 'An hour would give me time to find someone else to represent Mario. Will you let me have word one way or the other by Wednesday at nine o'clock?'

'Yes,' promised Roger.

She rose to her feet, her expression even brighter, and clasped his hand with both of hers.

'You're very kind and understanding,' she said. 'Thank you *very* much. And now I must go. I've taken up far too much of your time already.'

He showed her to the door and she stepped along the path too quickly for him to reach and open the gate for her. He did not want to attract much attention from his neighbours, so he turned back into the house. It was too early to reach any kind of conclusion, but he had become very predisposed towards helping the girl.

But supposing he did, and it were found out? What would Trevillion do or say? What would be his chances of staying in the Force, and what would be the result if he didn't? If he were dismissed ignominiously, would he still be eligible for the Allsafe job?

Supposing he checked that with Artemeus before he made a decision?

He thrust the thought aside. He hadn't even decided whether to tell Janet about the offer, hadn't decided whether he wanted the job, good though it was. He had to decide on the strength of his feeling for or against the Yard, not on one issue which was a long way from being typical. There were short term things he had to do; among them, see Rapelli.

But first, the Yard.

He heard Janet hurrying down the stairs, went to the foot of them and called, 'Can I give you a lift?'

'Oh, darling, if you would.' Janet's eyes lit up. 'I'm going to a committee meeting at the Town Hall, if you could just drop me off there.'

Ten minutes later he leaned across and opened the door for her, vividly reminded of doing exactly that for Maisie Dunster only a few hours ago, only a few hundred yards away from here. He did not dwell on that, but drove quickly to the Yard through thick traffic. The day was warm, the exhaust fumes were strong, it was the kind of day when anyone who had to work indoors was likely to be bad-tempered.

There was a kind of lethargy about the Yard, and a noticeable slackness among both senior and junior officials who were in the passages. With Coppell on the spot no one slouched, few groups gathered in the passages, but with Coppell away ...

Roger wondered whether he himself would behave any differently in such circumstances, and decided that Coppell or no Coppell, he would behave in exactly the same way. Wasn't that what most of this trouble was about?

Danizon, jacket off, was in his, Roger's, office.

'Good morning, sir,' he welcomed. 'Still all clear. Very little of any kind has come in during the night.' He pushed a thin file closer to Roger as he sat down. 'Like some coffee, sir?'

'No, thanks,' Roger said, and opened the report folder.

Maisie Dunster hadn't stirred from her flat according to two divisional men detailed to watch her. They had been relieved at eight o'clock and their place taken by others.

Pearson had gone home and had a tremendous quarrel with his wife; but neither of them had left the house since.

The post mortem on Ricardo Verdi showed that death had come from cerebral haemorrhage following a blow with a blunt instrument, compatible with an electric guitar.

The post mortem on Wilfred Smithson showed that death had followed multiple injuries to the head, chest and stomach, likely to be caused by being struck by a moving car.

There was as yet nothing to suggest that Verdi and Rapelli were old friends or associates, or even that they had known each other. There was plenty of evidence that Maisie Dunster had known both, however; some that Verdi as well as Rapelli had received her favours. As far as the police could find out, only two persons had known practically all the people involved. One was Patrick Fogarty and the other was Maisie. Yet there were no new revelations about either. The main inexplicable factor, however, was that Hamish Campbell had switched sides with such alacrity. Had Rachel Warrender been right? Had he been bribed? If so, how had Rachel—or her enquiry agent—discovered what the police, so far, had failed to discover? There was another question which, deliberately, he had not asked for. Did she know that Rapelli had planned to attack Verdi, even arranging his 'alibi' in advance?

Roger pondered these questions, soaked up all that was new in the reports, then put his head round the door of Danizon's office, and said, 'I'm going over to Brixton to see Rapelli.' He closed the door on Danizon's 'Right, sir.' Danizon would warn the authorities at the prison that he was on the way and Rapelli would probably be out of his cell and in one of the interviewing rooms at the front of the building.

He was at Brixton at a little before one o'clock.

Keys clanked, steel-capped boots clattered on cobbles, even in the sunlight the walls looked grim and grey. The big open courtyard was comparatively cool and the first big hall into which Roger was taken was almost chilly.

So was Rapelli's manner.

He looked fit and rested, and there was a haughtiness about him which Roger hadn't noticed before. He denied bribing Maisie or anyone else. He denied being at the Doon Club. He denied striking Verdi over the head. He denied everything.

'Whoever has told you these things is a liar,' he said flatly.

'But we can prove beyond doubt that you were at the Doon Club,' Roger insisted.

'No one, not even the great Superintendent West, can prove what isn't true,' said Rapelli. 'Whoever was there, it was not I.'

'Where are you getting the money from?' demanded Roger.

'I have no money. Miss Warrender made no charge for her help, and the other people are liars.' Rapelli's voice was pleasant-sounding but just now tinged with bitterness. 'The biggest liar is the woman, Dunster. I was with her before the others came in. First she admitted that, then she told a lie. Why don't you go and worry her with your questions? You might get the truth out of her if you try.'

Roger left the prison at ten minutes to two, wholly dissatisfied. Now the weather was not only hot but sultry and he thought he heard thunder in the distance, while the sky was a metallic blue. He drove towards Westminster Bridge in thick traffic, and was at the far side, waiting at the traffic lights which protected the approach to Parliament Square when he heard his name on the crackling radio. A dozen other names had been almost inaudible, but he recognised his own in a flash, and switched to *Information*.

'This is Superintendent West,' he said. 'I am at Parliament Square heading for the Yard. Will the message keep?'

'I doubt if you'll think so, sir,' *Information* said. 'A flash has just come in from division that Maisie Dunster has been found in her apartment, badly injured. A pretty messy business, they say.'

Roger felt himself going cold, and it was some time before he answered, roughly, 'I'll go to her flat right away.'

Chapter Sixteen

DYING STATEMENT

As Roger turned into the terrace where Maisie lived, an ambulance appeared from the other direction, white and shining. There were four police cars, three of them double-parked. Roger pulled up behind the third and jumped out, becoming one of a crowd of thirty or forty people being pushed back by two policemen. Men and women were at windows and doorways and gates; there was even a youth on a roof.

'Back a few yards, please,' one policeman was intoning. 'Make room for the ambulance, please.'

'Make room ... Back a few yards ... Make room ...'

Roger pushed his way through the crowd which was showing neither resentment nor eagerness at being pushed back. He found himself confronted by a massive policeman whose huge hand was spread out, palm outwards; he touched but did not push Roger.

'Please go back, sir.'

'All right, constable, let me through,' Roger ordered.

'If you're a relative—' The man turned a big, weather-browned face towards him. Recognising Roger, his eyebrows rose comically. 'Oh, Superintendent! Please pass through, sir.'

Two ambulance men were on their way across the small garden with its table-smooth lawn; there were no flower beds. A policeman stood at the front door. Suddenly, pushed out ahead of the ambulance men, was a big, lean, hungry-looking man with high and shiny cheekbones and a big and shiny nose. This was the Divisional Superintendent, Abe Court. He had big eyes with stubby eyelashes so black that it almost looked as if he wore eye shadow.

He espied Roger.

'Hallo, Superintendent.' He shook hands.

'Hallo,' said Roger. 'How is she?'

'Not a chance,' Court answered grimly. 'The doc's with her now, and she's asking for you.' As they went upstairs in the wake of the ambulance men Court went on, 'Doc wants to give her a sedative, but I persuaded him to wait until you got here.'

Roger nodded. While the ambulance men were manoeuvring their stretcher up the narrow stairs, he slipped past them, and into Maisie's room. A woman stood on one side of the bed, a man was bending over the other.

As Roger neared them, he saw Maisie's head and face.

From the eyes downwards she appeared uninjured, but her forehead and her fair hair were a bloodied, broken, tangled mess. Roger gulped as he reached the doctor's side. The girl's eyes, so brilliant and seductive last night, were swollen and bloodshot. Yet obviously she recognised him, and she turned her head.

'*Two minutes,*' the police surgeon said. He held a hypodermic syringe, already loaded.

Roger nodded, went down on one knee, and took Maisie's limp hand.

'Who was it?' Roger asked, in a whisper.

She moistened her lips, and the woman moved from the other side of the bed and moistened them with a sponge.

'Just give me his name,' Roger urged.

'You—won't believe me,' she muttered.

'Never mind whether I'll believe you,' Roger said. 'Maisie, I'm terribly sorry. And the quicker I know the quicker we can get you to hospital and—'

He actually saw a movement at her lips.

'Waste of time,' she said. 'I'm done for. It was—Mario.'

'Mario Rapelli?' he echoed, incredulously.

'There you are,' she said. 'You don't believe me.' She closed her eyes. 'I didn't know there were such things as —good cops. Give me a kiss—Handsome.'

The doctor had gone to the other side of the bed, the woman rolled up the girl's sleeve, and Roger stood up and bent over her and kissed her lightly. Quite deliberately she opened her mouth, and he rested his lips on hers for a long moment. There were movements which he saw out of the corner of his eyes, and suddenly her lips, her face, her whole body went limp.

He stood up.

The doctor was putting the needle into its box, the woman and one ambulance driver were wrapping sheeting round Maisie's head. Her eyes were closed, and he felt as sure as a man could be that she would never open them again.

*　　*　　*

Half an hour later, Roger was back at the Yard. For once, he wished Coppell were in his office; he wanted to discuss the situation with the commander. He went straight to his own office, and told Danizon, whose look of astonishment was almost boyish.

'But Rapelli was at Brixton all night!'

'Yes,' Roger said. 'One place he couldn't have got away from. There are three possibilities,' he went on in a clipped voice. 'First, that Rapelli has a twin or a double. Second, that Maisie lied on her deathbed. Third, that she genuinely mistook her assailant for Rapelli. I don't favour one idea against the other yet.' He dropped into the chair behind his desk. 'Superintendent Court is handling the routine from division. There's no trace of a break-in, and it looks as if the killer got in over the roof. Abe Court is checking the two divisional men supposed to be watching her. Whoever attacked her had a key to her room, possibly the house. The weapon was a hammer, taken from a cupboard in the room: it was under her bed and there were no fingerprints on the handle. Time of attack hasn't been determined but it seems likely that it was around four o'clock, according to the thickness of the coagulation of the blood. She was found by one of her friends—Cleo, one of the would-be witnesses for Mario Rapelli—who couldn't understand why she wasn't up. They had a hairdressing appointment together. There's a caretaker and general factotum in the house and he let this Cleo in with a master key.' Roger saw the glint in Danizon's eyes, and shook his head. 'The key was on a bunch which weighs about half a pound and hangs on the head of the caretaker's bed. Not a chance that was the key that was used.' He paused, as Danizon finished writing, and went on, 'Can you make a brief report from that, and start the file?'

'Yes, sir.'

'Thanks. Any messages?'

'They're on your desk,' answered Danizon. 'Your wife called just before you came in but she said it wasn't urgent.'

Janet seldom called during the day; Roger wondered what it was about, but put it out of his mind.

Opening the top file, he saw several telephone messages. Not only Janet but Benjamin Artemeus had called, and a Harold Phillipson, of the *Globe*. *Phillipson*. He was the managing editor of the paper, and had certainly approved even if he hadn't written the article so critical of him, Roger, and the Yard. The message ran, *Can Superinten-*

dent West please call before one-thirty?

It was now nearly a quarter to two.

Roger put a call in to the newspaper, running over the details of the article, wondering again why Janet had called and what Artemeus wanted. And he was sharply reminded of the fact that he had not told Janet of the offer from Allsafe. The next moment his telephone rang and the operator said, 'Mr. Phillipson, sir.'

'Thanks. Mr. Phillipson?'

'Good afternoon, Superintendent.' The editor had a deep, pleasing voice with a strangely sardonic intonation, with the emphasis on the 'good' and the 'super'. 'I'm very glad you've called.'

'I've just got in from Chelsea,' Roger said. 'I saw Maisie Dunster.'

'The young woman who really began all this,' Phillipson observed. 'She died on the way to hospital. Did you know?'

Roger didn't answer at once. He had been sure it was inevitable but still had a sense of shock. He was disturbed, too, because Phillipson had known before him.

There was a perfunctory tap on the door, and Danizon put his head into the room.

'I thought you should know that Maisie Dunster is dead, sir. She died on the way to hospital.'

'Yes,' Roger said. 'Thanks.' As the door closed on Danizon he turned back to Phillipson. 'I'm sorry, someone came into the office. Yes, I know about Maisie. I hope you know that I won't rest until we've found her murderer.'

There was a long pause, before Phillipson answered.

'A good case could be made out for blaming the Yard for allowing her to be murdered, you know—particularly since she was a key witness in Rapelli's defence.'

'Mr. Phillipson,' Roger said evenly, 'no one is more keenly aware than I that we fell down on the job of watching her, but we are not legally responsible. Do you really want to make our investigation more difficult by throwing mud at us in your columns? Whether we're wrong or right, some of it always sticks.'

'Sometimes it should,' Phillipson retorted. He still spoke with that sardonic intonation as if he were laughing at himself, at Roger or the situation. 'However, I don't propose to throw any more, but that isn't what I wanted to talk about. I'm not sure we should talk over the telephone. Could you come and see me this afternoon?'

Roger hesitated. The editor of a national newspaper would not ask him to give up his time unless it were worthwhile. He wanted to interview the men who had been watching Maisie, and he wanted to concentrate on Rapelli, but neither was of urgent importance.

'Yes,' he answered. 'About two-thirty.'

'I'll be glad to see you,' said Phillipson. 'Thank you.'

Roger rang off, and immediately put a call in to Janet, but there was no answer; she must have gone shopping or to one of her afternoon committee meetings. He called Artemeus, at Allsafe, half-expecting to find the man out at lunch. But no; he answered the company operator's ring.

'Ah, Mr. West. Thank you very much for calling,' he said. 'I'm particularly anxious to see you about a most unexpected development. Could you possibly spare half an hour this afternoon?'

It never rained but it poured. However, he should be away from the *Globe*'s office at about three or three-fifteen, however, and would be fairly near the Allsafe offices in the Strand. There was no reason why he shouldn't look in, although every reason why Artemeus should not think him at the security company's beck and call. But making a prestige issue was pointless now.

'I could look in briefly about three-thirty,' he said. 'Perhaps a little earlier.'

'How *very* kind! I'll be in my office and free from three o'clock onwards, and I won't make any appointments until you've been. I *do* appreciate it.' Artemeus was almost effusive.

Roger rang off, and called Danizon.

'I want a car right away, for Fleet Street and the Strand,' he said. 'I'll be out for about two hours altogether.'

'Right, sir! I'll fix it.'

Roger rang off again, and opened the Rapelli file, glanced through it, then put it in his black portfolio. Next he called Abe Court, who was a very brusque man on the telephone, one who always gave the impression that he couldn't wait to ring off.

'Handsome? ... I've a little more information but not much. Those two men we had on Maisie were diverted —there was an emergency call to Martin's Bank in the High Street, and they were almost on the spot, so they took a chance. They arrested the bank raiders too—a couple who would have escaped if they hadn't arrived when they did. Hardly the point, I suppose, two thieves in custody and one life lost, but that killing could have been an inside job. No certainty my chaps were to blame ... They're very cut up about it. Want to see them here or at the Yard? I've got 'em here for you.'

'The Yard,' Roger said. 'Four-thirty.'

'Right, Handsome. They're both good men, don't forget.'

Roger thought bleakly as he rang off: and Maisie is dead. Nevertheless, he was glad that Abe Court fought for his men, and God knew he was the last man to condemn an officer for using his own judgment in an emergency. He picked up the Fogarty file, which was very thin, and the file on Hamish Campbell, which was not much thicker. He put these in the portfolio, also.

A new Rover was outside the main entrance with a youthful, very blond, young detective officer standing by the door. His colouring reminded Roger vividly of Maisie's fair hair, so spattered and soaked in blood.

'Good afternoon, sir.' The man opened the door.

'Hallo, Ashe.' Roger got inside, and waited for the other to get at the wheel before adding, 'The *Globe* offices, park the car as near as you can and stand where you can keep me in sight. I might be out in twenty minutes.'

'Right, sir.'

The *Globe*'s offices were nearly brand new, very modern, and in an off-white which nevertheless reflected the glare of the sun. Fleet Street's narrow roadway was jammed with cars, cabs and huge red buses; one was so used to them, Roger thought, it was difficult to see them as a major cause of London's traffic problems. The pavements on either side were thronged, too; why did girls look so much prettier and more provocative in sleeveless cotton dresses? There was a space outside the newspaper's offices, and a doorman in a puce-coloured uniform came forward smartly.

'Superintendent West, sir?'

'Yes.'

'The young lady on the right as you go in will take you up to Mr. Phillipson, sir.'

The 'young lady' was in a puce-coloured dress with a very short skirt, and she had long and shapely legs. Her face was more pert than pretty. She led Roger to a small lift, obviously reserved for V.I.P.s, and within two minutes he was in the long, narrow office of the editor. The walls were of marble or mock-marble, the floor was covered from wall to wall in tufted black carpet. A few plaques of past editors were on the walls. At one end of the room was a horseshoe-shaped conference table with ten or twelve places, at the other an enormous desk with

Phillipson behind it, his back to the window, and several comfortable-looking armchairs in front. There were some very modern upright chairs, too.

Phillipson stood up. He was tall, distinguished-looking, and silver-haired, a very lean man in a beautifully cut suit. He did not round the desk but extended his arm across it; after they had shaken hands he motioned to one of the easy chairs.

'Do sit down, Superintendent.'

'May I have one of these?' Roger took an upright chair which was at the side of the desk, and this way he could see Phillipson without having the sun in his eyes; and Phillipson did not have him in such a searching light and at the slight disadvantage of being in a semi-recumbent position.

Phillipson smiled but did not comment.

'I asked you to come because I have a report—a well-authenticated report from a highly reliable source, I may say—which directly concerns you,' he said. 'In some cases I would print the story as fair comment, but this one is so personal that, as you said over the telephone, some of the—ah—mud would stick even if we printed a denial the next day. I thought that in view of our somewhat strained relations this week, it might be wise to discuss the report with you first.'

He waited long enough for Roger to comment, but Roger stayed silent. A door near Phillipson opened and a fluffy-haired, middle-aged woman in a dark dress came in with a trolley on which were coffee, brandy, liqueurs and cigars. The soft treatment, Roger reflected drily.

'White or black coffee, sir?'

'Khaki, please.'

'Thank you.' She poured out, offered him sugar, poured out for Phillipson, and left them.

'Brandy?' Phillipson asked.

No thanks,' said Roger. 'I haven't much time and I would like to know the details of this report, please.'

'Very well.' Phillipson picked up a thin sheaf of papers, without glancing at them. 'This is prepared by my chief correspondent, who has concentrated on it with three reporters, for two days. I have a copy here for you. It states, very simply, that you are likely to be placed under suspension before the week is out; that, if suspended, you will resign; that some of your somewhat arrogant behaviour in the past few days is due to the fact that you have a most attractive offer of a post in a private security company, at four times your salary in the Metropolitan Police. The implication is that you have deliberately ridden rough-shod over police rules and regulations so as to precipitate a crisis in which you would be dismissed or could resign without any loss of—ah—dignity and respect. If you simply resigned to take a more paying job you would lose the respect not only of your colleagues but of a great many of the general public. If, however, you resigned as a protest against the autocratic methods being adopted at the Yard, largely by the new commissioner, you would retain the goodwill both of police and public.'

Phillipson stopped; and the room seemed hushed. There was not even a rustling of paper, no sound from outside. Then Phillipson stood up, making himself a silhouette against the big window behind him, looked out over Fleet Street and towards Ludgate Circus and St. Paul's, and went on very quietly, 'I hope you agree that you should have an opportunity to refute any of these statements, Superintendent. As this is prepared as a major feature for tomorrow's issue, it has to be set and carefully proof-read, as well as checked by our legal departments to make sure that any libel read into it can be defended on the grounds of fair comment. That is why I asked you to come this afternoon. What is your comment, Superintendent?'

Chapter Seventeen

ULTIMATUM?

Roger leaned forward and took the document from Phillipson's hand. He glanced through it, more to give himself time to think than because he needed to know more than Phillipson had told him. There were about eight, sparsely typewritten pages, and several photographs: one of him, one of Vice-Admiral Trevillion, one of New Scotland Yard, one of an Allsafe Security van standing outside a factory, and finally one of him with Janet and the boys, a happy picture taken about ten years ago.

He looked up.

'You know,' he said, 'this seems remarkably like an ultimatum: refute every statement here or we print.'

'You could regard it in that light,' agreed Phillipson, urbanely.

'What exactly would you like—or hope for—me to do?'

'I have no preferences,' answered Phillipson. 'If you are able to give a categorical denial of the story then I would not print it. If however you are prepared to confirm it in part or whole, I would print it in its entirety. *Can* you deny the report, Superintendent?'

Roger looked at him levelly, hoping that nothing in his expression gave away the tension which he felt. He was so angry that it was difficult to be calm, but calm he had to be. He folded the report around the photographs, and the packet was just small enough to fit into the side pocket of his jacket.

'Quite apart from my personal involvement, there is a major issue here,' he stated carefully.

'I would be glad to hear it.'

'Someone at the Yard has been giving you—or your correspondent—confidential information.' Roger drank his coffee, put the cup down, and then shifted from the hardback chair to one of the armchairs. The soft cushions seemed to enfold him and when he stretched his legs and leaned his head back, he both felt like and was a picture of extreme comfort. 'The someone must hold a position of great trust, obviously.'

'Ah,' said Phillipson. 'Such as you.'

'None of that story has come from me,' asserted Roger.

'As a policeman, would you find that easy to prove?' asked Phillipson.

'I would find it easy to sue for libel, and leave you to prove justification,' Roger retorted.

All of his doubts faded as he spoke. This man was out to get him, and had been from the start. Phillipson had enormous self-confidence and the great prestige and money of a powerful newspaper behind him, and obviously he would not carry out such a vendetta without his board knowing, and approving. This wasn't simply an editor getting on his high horse over what he considered to be a public scandal; it was a deliberate attempt to discredit him, Superintendent Roger West.

What possible motive could there be?

'As a policeman,' Roger went on, 'I would keep my evidence and my methods of investigation to myself, until the time came to defend.' He looked up at the other, whom he could hardly see because of the bright window light, and did not move for a long time. Phillipson was obviously determined to wait until he spoke again before commenting.

Roger put his hands on the arms of the chair, loosely at first, but suddenly gripping with both hands and using all the strength of his arms, so that he positively leapt to his feet. He startled Phillipson, who backed away sharply.

'Well, we'll soon see,' Roger finished. 'I really mustn't stay.'

'But surely—' began Phillipson.

'Good afternoon,' Roger said, smiling brightly. 'Will the young lady who brought me up here see me back to the foyer? Or shall I find my own way down?'

He matched Phillipson's wide-eyed astonishment with a smile, and turned towards the door. For a few seconds he thought that the man would let him go, but suddenly Phillipson moved and came hurrying after him.

'Superintendent! Unless you can satisfy me that these assertions are untrue I shall publish, and your reputation will be at stake.'

As suddenly, Roger stopped; then, very slowly, he turned round. Phillipson was close to him, astonishment and perhaps alarm written all over his face. Obviously he was completely flummoxed by Roger's reaction.

'Mr. Phillipson,' Roger said. 'You are the editor of this newspaper and in law you and you alone are responsible for any statement it publishes. You cannot shift that responsibility on to others, most certainly not on to me. Whether you publish that story is entirely a matter for you. As a police officer I can only tell you that in my view the story proves that there is a serious leakage of information at Scotland Yard, and if I were asked by my supervisors what course to take I would advise them to begin a thorough investigation into the leakage. I would also recommend that if any evidence of bribery or corruption were produced—that is, if it could be established that the information was bought from an officer or servant of the Metropolitan Police, action should be taken both against the supplier of the information *and* against the person who gave the bribe or who encouraged and/or authorised it.'

He paused, drawing a deep breath, looking much angrier even than he felt.

'As a private individual,' he went on, 'I would wait for the result of official action before suing for damages. I hope you're *very* clear on how I regard this form of blackmail.'

He turned on his heel, speaking again as he reached the door.

'As for the report, I'm going to take it forthwith to the commander of the C.I.D. and I shall ask him to show it to the commissioner immediately. I am sure that both will be fascinated by the half-truths as well as by the outright lies.'

He went out, letting the door swing to behind him.

*　　*　　*

He would do exactly as he had said, he knew, as he went down in the main lift, but letting fly as he had didn't actually help. He needed to find out what this was all about, why this vendetta had been started. His position would be enormously strengthened if he could take some evidence to Coppell, but there wasn't much likelihood of being able to do that. There was a very grave danger that he would be so preoccupied by this that he would not be able to concentrate on the investigation into Maisie's murder. As a man he hated the report; as a policeman and as a man, he had to find that killer.

He had a sudden mental image of Maisie, lying so near to death.

'*You won't believe me.*' And a moment later, '*It was Mario.*' And then, '*There you are. You don't believe me.*' And soon, '*Give me a kiss, Handsome.*'

He could imagine the feel of the moist warmth of her lips.

Detective Officer Ashe came up, smartly.

'I'm just along here, sir. I—' He broke off, looking concerned. 'Are you all right?'

Roger looked at him vaguely as they walked on.

'Er, yes, I'm fine.' He got into the car and the puce-uniformed doorman hovered. Should he go to see Artemeus in such a mood as this? he wondered. It was on the way to the Yard, he needn't stay long, and if he didn't go he would fidget on and off for hours wondering what the Allsafe man wanted. As they were edging out into a stream of traffic, a bus roared by within inches of the Rover, making two or three pedestrians leap out of the way. 'Get his number,' Roger snapped, and Ashe, quick off the mark, called out the number of the bus over the radio-telephone.

'Could have crashed into us *and* killed a couple of people,' Ashe complained.

'Not often you get a bad bus driver,' remarked Roger. 'Do you know the Allsafe offices in the Strand?'

'Yes, sir.'

'Take me there, please.'

Something, he couldn't quite place what it was, told him that Ashe was startled by the order. There was rivalry as well as co-operation between Allsafe and the Metropolitan Police, he remembered—then pushed the thought to the back of his mind. The near accident and the flashback to Maisie had helped him recover from his anger at the newspaper editor's near-threat. But why the hell should they set out to discredit him? Who had he offended? Was it concerned with a case he had investigated—or was investigating? This one, perhaps? But speculation was useless, except that it sometimes set the subconscious mind working. Roger gave a mental shrug to his shoulders and tried to relax for a few moments as they passed first Aldwych, then Waterloo Bridge Road, and, a few moments later, turned right.

A doorman was waiting; a young lad took him up to Artemeus's office. Artemeus was in a long, panelled room, with an oval conference table and an oak, leather-topped desk, very like that at the *Globe*. As he stood up to greet Roger, a door opened behind the desk, there was a clink of china, and a woman came in wheeling a tea-trolley laden with teapot, cups and saucers, a plate of thinly cut sandwiches and another of eclairs. Artemeus was smiling, pleased, possibly even smug.

'Very good of you to come, Mr. West ... I didn't want to trouble you but a stipulation has arisen which I didn't anticipate ... Milk? ... Just a little milk for Mr. West, Nora ... And what I had imagined would be a very relaxed period of contemplation has, I fear, become a matter of urgency ... That's all, Nora, thank you.'

He stopped speaking and looked straight at Roger, and now his amiability seemed to melt away; here was someone who knew exactly what he wanted and how to get it. Those grey eyes were piercing, and there was a hardness in them which betrayed the true nature of the man.

Roger waited.

'One of our competitor firms has made a bid for our shares,' Artemeus announced. 'It is a substantial bid, and our shareholders are likely to accept unless we can offer them something better. There are two other firms, as you know, who are of some importance in this field. If we took *them* over, we would be in a position not only to remain independent but also to buy out the main competitor in the field, the one who wants to buy us. Need I tell you how important the issues are?'

'You want a monopoly in the private security organisations,' Roger remarked dryly.

'Exactly.' Artemeus let a kind of shield fall over his eyes, hiding their hardness, and stretched a languid hand for an eclair. 'In normal circumstances I would not have been so frank, Mr. West, but the situation is so urgent that I really have no choice. You will no doubt guess that the take-over offer came unexpectedly. It will be announced in the evening newspapers tonight, and you would have seen at once why we are so anxious to have your services.'

Roger said heavily, 'Spell it out for me, please.'

'Very well.' Artemeus took a sip of tea, and leaned forward earnestly. 'If you are with us, Mr. West, we can merge with the smaller companies. They are equally impressed with your importance, your account-pulling power. If you are not with us, then—' he shrugged his shoulders '—then we shall be taken over. This is really very simple; the ways of big business are usually simple.' When Roger did not answer at once, Artemeus went on, 'There is another point of view which you would be well to consider. *Your* position. You are at this moment in a position to dictate terms. If you wanted double the money I offered, I think my board would be prepared to pay.'

His words seemed to fall on to deaf ears. Roger stared at him but did not speak. He believed that he could understand a great many things which had been obscured until he had come here: certainly he saw a glimmering of new and vivid light. But he wanted time to think, to check some facts—and he needed to keep this man in a good humour as he checked them. For as long as he thought that he might join Allsafe, Artemeus would be blandly pleasant and helpful.

Then, as if aware of uncertainty and tension, Artemeus went on, 'If you have doubts, Mr. West, why don't you talk it over with your wife? She sounded very charming when I spoke to her on the telephone this morning.'

Every muscle in Roger's body went stiff, and for a moment Artemeus looked alarmed.

'You mean you told my wife about this offer?'

'I—well—I—yes,' said Artemeus, his voice suddenly unsteady. 'I—er—I called the Yard this morning and—I —they said you were at home. So I called—*West*. What is the matter? What are you—'

Roger was on his feet and leaning across the desk. One part of his mind was aware of the cold rage in him and the need for self-control, the other was aware of the fear —the near-terror—on this man's face. Roger forced himself to stand upright as Artemeus craned back in his chair, hands raised as if he expected physical violence.

'What did you tell her?' Roger grated.

'I—er—I simply said that circumstances enabled me to—er—improve substantially on my previous offer. Good God, West, don't tell me you hadn't told her! I took that for granted.' He broke off, swallowing hard. 'I really had no idea—'

'You cold-blooded liar,' growled Roger. 'You found out she didn't know and you told her so as to put more pressure on me. You're so anxious to make your miserable profit you'll try any trick.'

He moved swiftly, rounding the desk in three strides. Artemeus rose in his chair, then dropped down again, for there was no room to pass. Roger gripped him by the shoulders and shook him to and fro, slowly, deliberately, menacingly. His fingers bit into the man's fleshy shoulders, and Artemeus winced with pain.

'Are you behind the *Globe*'s campaign? Are you trying to get me thrown out of the Yard or forced to resign so that I have to come to you and take your filthy money? Is that it?' He shook the man to each of the words and Artemeus's head bobbed to and fro. 'Tell me the truth or I'll shake your head off your shoulders.'

That was when the door near the desk opened, and Phillipson of the *Globe* came in. He closed the door quietly, and stepped towards Roger, who did not release his hold on Artemeus, just turned his head and glared.

'If you do that, West, you'll have earned another big headline,' Phillipson said. 'Let Artemeus go.'

Chapter Eighteen

THREAT

For a long time, it seemed, Roger stood unmoving, while Phillipson's words echoed and re-echoed in his mind. Then he relinquished his hold on Artemeus, and the man fell back into his chair, gasping for breath. Phillipson, his calm and assured self for a few moments, gave him a sideways glance and seemed to become momentarily alarmed. Artemeus's breath was coming in short gasps, and he was heaving, as if breathing were painful and shallow. Phillipson went closer to the desk, on the other side from Roger, and pressed a bell. Immediately, a woman said, 'Yes, sir?'

'Miss Noble, doesn't Mr. Artemeus have some tablets for his heart condition?' Phillipson asked.

'Yes, sir,' answered Miss Noble. 'He keeps them in a snuff-box in his left-hand pocket. Shall I bring in some water?'

'There's milk here,' observed Phillipson. 'The next time I ring, I want you to play back that tape.'

Roger put his hand into Artemeus's left-hand pocket and took out a small, flat box, silver-coloured. He opened this as Phillipson poured out some milk into Artemeus's cup. Roger went behind the gasping man and gently eased his head backwards, while Phillipson put a small tablet to the parted lips, and ordered firmly, 'Take this tablet, Ben.'

Artemeus opened his mouth and swallowed hard; the tablet disappeared.

'Now drink some milk.'

Artemeus drank; gulp, gulp, gulp. Phillipson drew back, putting the cup down, while Roger slid the small box back into the sick man's pocket. The harsh breathing seemed to ease at once, but a bluish tinge at his lips grew rather worse. After a few moments, Phillipson leaned forward and rang again. Almost at once, voices sounded, and suddenly Roger recognised his own.

'*Tell me the truth or I'll shake your head off your shoulders.*' The restrained fury could not be disguised.

'Go back a little further,' Phillipson ordered into the speaker.

Roger walked swiftly to the desk. Since Artemeus's mention of Janet he had hardly thought, just reacted—first to his own anger, then to Phillipson's calmness and control. But now he knew exactly what to do. Ignoring Phillipson's astonished stare, ignoring the metallic twang of his and Artemeus's recorded voices, he picked up the telephone and dialled a number.

'Scotland Yard,' an operator answered.

'Detective Sergeant Danizon,' Roger said. He saw Phillipson's eyes widen, saw the man's assurance wilting. 'Hallo, Tom. I want you to send four men to the offices of the Allsafe Security Company in the Strand. They are to come straight up to the office of Mr. Artemeus—Benjamin Artemeus. I will be here to give them instructions ... No, don't ring off yet! I want an immediate check on the directors of all the major private security corporations; you'd better make that senior directors as well as directors ... Yes ... I want to find out if there is any association between any of them and Mario Rapelli, Maisie Dunster, or Hamish Campbell, in fact with any of the people concerned in the Verdi affair. It's very urgent,' he went on. 'Get it started, and I'll come back as soon as I can and talk to the commander to see that we get it done tonight ... Get those four men over here from the nearest patrols.'

He rang off. Artemeus was sitting back in his chair, his breathing very much easier. Phillipson was still staring, open-mouthed. Roger poured himself out some more tea and helped himself to an eclair.

'What good do you think this will do you?' demanded Phillipson, his voice suddenly shrill. 'When I tell your superiors that you used violence on Artemeus, you will be through at the Yard.'

'Possibly,' Roger said coldly. 'Has it ever occurred to you to put the public good above your own?'

'Don't be a smug hypocrite!'

'Oh, no,' Roger said. 'I'm not a hypocrite. I'm hot-headed at times and at others I cut corners and get myself into trouble, but I always work for the public good. That's my job. You're the hypocrite here. You run a newspaper supposedly in the public interest, yet use it to try to influence the activity of the police force and to smear the character of police officers.'

Phillipson said, 'You must be bluffing.'

'He—he is,' said Artemeus in a choky voice. 'He—he—he'll play if you offer him enough.' His voice was thin and wheezy, but his colour was better and he sat up in his chair. 'A—a hundred thousand pounds, West—tax free. Just forget this clash of ideas, and—and join us.'

'This, as you call it, is now part of the official record,' said Roger coolly. 'I don't yet know exactly what's going on but I do know it will soon stop.' He now felt in complete control of the situation. 'You would both be well advised to make a full and truthful statement.'

'A—a hundred and *fifty* thousand,' Artemeus gasped. 'Tax *free*.'

'Maisie Dunster was murdered this morning,' Roger said coldly. 'Ricardo Verdi was murdered last Wednesday. If you can tell me why, here's your chance to justify your attitude. If you can't or won't I shall take you both to Scotland Yard for questioning and possible charge.'

'You've nothing to charge us with,' Phillipson protested thinly.

'Attempting to bribe a policeman in the course of his duty—'

'No one would ever believe it!'

Roger moved with devastating speed, reached the door, opened it and barked, 'Miss Noble. Was the tape still recording when Mr. Artemeus came round?'

The woman was sitting at a desk with several telephones, a small push-button telephone control board, and several tape-recorders, all of these in slots at the side of her desk, all of them playing. She moved her hand as if to stop one but Roger rasped, 'Don't touch that.'

He strode forward.

'Which is the recorder for the other room?' She pointed a quivering finger towards it. 'Don't touch it,' Roger ordered. 'I know you work for Mr. Artemeus, but if you obstruct me in any way you will be an accomplice to him and an accessory to everything these men have done.'

She dropped back into her chair.

Roger looked at the tape-recorder, which was marked 'Mr Artemeus'; so the woman had told the truth, he thought. Glancing back into the room through the wide open door, he saw the two men staring after him; they looked appalled. He took another step forward, thinking that the four Yard men should be here soon, that he hadn't much further to go. He wasn't sure of the strength of his case, wasn't at all sure of the details, but he did know that he had become involved through none of his own causing in a struggle for the monopoly of private security forces in the country. Warned by a sixth sense, he looked back yet again, and this time saw Phillipson spring towards the open doorway, a gun in his hand. Roger did not move, except to throw a glance over his shoulder at Miss Noble, who might already be so involved that she was virtually compelled to help both Phillipson and Artemeus. Phillipson drew a pace nearer but was still further away from Roger than Artemeus, who was sitting motionless at his desk, but must be aware of the gun in his associate's hand.

'Phillipson,' Roger said, 'put that gun down.'

Phillipson advanced a step closer. He looked very pale and his eyes glittered.

'One hundred and fifty thousand pounds for your co-operation,' he said in a low rasping voice, 'or I shall kill you.'

*   *   *

Roger did not doubt that the man meant it. In the tone of his voice, in his manner, there was all the indication needed. For the second time in a few days he was at the business end of a gun. Again, his thoughts flashed to Maisie, but they did not linger. He was face to face with disaster at a time when the whole world seemed to be tumbling about him. Two appointments, fairly straightforward appointments with two highly reputable men, and he was confronting the leaders of the campaign against him.

He still did not understand why, but felt quite sure he was right. The menace of the gun was all too convincing.

'You heard me,' Phillipson grated.

'Yes,' Roger agreed. 'I heard you. One hundred and fifty thousand pounds to sell my soul, or else death by shooting.' How long would it be before the patrols got here, he wondered anxiously. He must play for time, and hope it wouldn't run out before they arrived. 'I always wanted to be rich,' he went on. 'Always. And I always wanted to be the boss. *Would* I be the boss of Allsafe?'

'Yes!' cried Artemeus. 'Yes, there would be no one else. You would be the administrative and executive chief, the commissioner and the commander C.I.D. rolled into one! And you'd get those holidays. You would have normal hours. When I told her this your wife was delighted.'

'I'm sure she was,' Roger said. Once again he felt that seething rage rise within him, but fought it down. 'What do I have to do to qualify for this high position and considerable fortune?'

'Withdraw those men you sent for,' ordered Phillipson. 'And then resign from the Yard at a Press Conference tonight.'

'Why tonight?' asked Roger.

'For God's sake use your head!' cried Artemeus. 'If you join us and all the newspapers have the story tomorrow none of our shareholders would accept the competitor's offer. That's all you have to do. Appear at a televised Press Conference and resign. We'll give you six months' advance on your salary, and you can have a month's holiday—*two* months' holiday.'

'It's too easy,' Roger said, half-laughing. 'It's far too good to be true.' Even to his ears his laughter sounded completely genuine. I should have been on the stage, he thought wryly. Then he thought: *When the devil are those four men coming?* They couldn't be long, now, it must be twenty minutes since he had telephoned Danizon, who would waste no time.

He sauntered back to Artemeus's office, aware of Miss Noble's heavy breathing, the whirring of the tape-recorder as every word they uttered was recorded. Phillipson still kept him covered with his gun, but did not seem so distressed, and Roger saw that Artemeus had a document of some kind on the desk in front of him. Artemeus had recovered remarkably well from that attack, he thought.

'You just have to sign this contract,' Artemeus said now. 'That's all.'

'And this confession,' added Phillipson.

'Ah—a confession sounds interesting,' said Roger casually. 'What have I done?'

'Killed Maisie Dunster,' Phillipson stated. So Phillipson and Artemeus were involved in the Verdi case, thought Roger grimly. This whole affair was obviously far, far deeper than he had realised. Exerting all his self-control to appear casual and unconcerned, he picked up the first document, and found it exactly what Phillipson had said: a short confession that he had attacked Maisie because she knew that he had been taking bribes and covering up the activities of notorious criminals. It was beautifully typed on paper from New Scotland Yard. How had they come by that?

'Sign that or I shall shoot you,' Phillipson's voice was steady.

Roger put his hand to his pocket, and there was a silent cry within him. *When are those four coming?* Phillipson lowered his arm and Artemeus handed him a pen with which to sign. Roger took this, poised it over the confession—and then, in a lightning movement, jerked it backwards and towards Phillipson's face. At the same time he leapt past Artemeus, twisting round as he did so. Phillipson was staggering back, the gun waving, but he would recover his balance before Roger could get at him, and there was only one thing left to do. Grabbing Artemeus's jacket with one hand so that the man was unable to move, he swivelled his chair round with the other, and crouched behind it. Phillipson steadied, the gun pointed, and suddenly a bullet spat; there was a *zutt* of sound and a stab of flame and a bullet buried itself in the big oak desk.

'Mind me!' screeched Artemeus.

Phillipson levelled the gun again, and moved to one side. Roger swivelled the chair slowly, tightening his grip on Artemeus, keeping his prisoner always between himself and the gun.

Phillipson fired again, and missed.

As he aimed a third time, the passage door burst open and two Yard men flung themselves into the room. They saw the gun and did not need Roger's shout of warning. Fast upon that, one of them yelled on a note of alarm that cut through Roger like a knife, '*Watch him, sir!*'

Watch who?

Watch Phillipson!

Suddenly Roger saw the newspaper editor fling himself towards the window, firing at the two Yard men as he did so. Reaching the window, he kicked the glass through with one foot, then hurled himself out to the pavement ten storeys below.

*   *   *

Benjamin Artemeus sat shivering in his chair, while Roger looked down at the sprawled figure on the pavement. In her office, Miss Noble sat at the desk, hands on her broad lap, hopelessness in her expression.

*   *   *

'If you don't mind me saying so, sir,' said Danizon, 'that was a wonderful job. I've talked to the secretary, Miss Noble, she says you were magnificent. Her very words, sir. And if you don't mind me saying so, you look all in.

And you'll have to see the commander and probably the commissioner very soon. Would it be a good idea if you rested for half an hour? There's a bathroom next door, and a room next to that where you could put your feet up.'

They were going through papers in Artemeus's desk.

They had already done a great deal since the shooting and the tragedy. Ambulances and police had arrived and Phillipson's body had been taken away. An area of the Strand had been roped off and the police were busy there. Other police had been sent to Phillipson's office, which had been sealed off, and members of the Board of the *Globe* as well as of Allsafe and other interested companies were being interviewed. Artemeus was now at the Yard. He had not spoken since Roger had arrested him, and was so blue in the face that he seemed likely to have a fatal attack at any moment. A police surgeon was standing by. Coppell had been interrupted at the European Police Conference, and he was believed to have told the commissioner about the situation.

There were at least two things Roger didn't know.

First, who *had* killed Maisie? Second, what part had Rapelli really played in the murder of Verdi, and why had Verdi been killed?

The answers were somewhere in this mass of papers; they could even be in the evidence he had already discovered, but which he could not interpret properly.

These things went through his mind as he said, 'Good idea, Tom. By the way, what brought you in person?'

'I took a chance after I'd ordered patrol cars to come here,' said Danizon, with refreshing honesty. 'Just for once I wanted to be out on a job. I—oh, I forgot. Your wife telephoned twice this afternoon, and I thought she sounded anxious. When you've had a shower you might like to call her.'

'Yes,' Roger said, heavily. 'I will.'

He went along to the bathroom, through a small and pleasantly furnished room where there were drinks, cocktail biscuits, glasses and some magazines—and a telephone. He thought he could guess what Janet had to say and he was in no mood, yet, to hear it. There was a lot to do, and soon he would have to report to Coppell—and quite possibly the commissioner as well.

Chapter Nineteen

INTERRUPTION

Roger soaked for a few minutes in the bath. The water was warm, too warm, but soothing to his over-tired body. Danizon was right, he thought. He must relax completely for ten minutes or so, must clear his mind of everything and forget the case entirely. He lay back and closed his eyes, but immediately he did so thoughts came crowding into his head—thoughts of Maisie, of Rachel Warrender, of Mario Rapelli, of Hamish Campbell, of everyone involved—each one forming a clear and living picture on the retina of his mind. Somewhere, in this maze of tangled evidence, were the clues he needed. Both Artemeus and Phillipson had obviously been involved in the campaign to discredit him in the Police Force and thus compel him to join Allsafe. But could that be simply to boost Allsafe against its competitors? Such a thought was inconceivable. And what in heaven's name, Roger wondered, was the connection with the Verdi affair?

If he had to point a finger at the most astonishing development in this whole case it would be Rachel Warrender's visit, and her pleading for him to find out the truth. She had been in a desperate mood, had not slept all night; it was strange that she had felt so deeply at such a simple deception.

'My God!' Roger suddenly exclaimed aloud.

He looked round, and saw a telephone. He grabbed it,

water dripping, instrument slipping from his fingers. An operator answered.

'Detective Sergeant Danizon, please. He's in Mr. Art—'

'I know where he is, sir.'

There was only a moment's pause before Danizon answered, but in this pause Roger's thoughts were racing, and he spoke as Danizon came on the line.

'Have you come across any documents or files showing who represents Allsafe legally?'

'Well, yes, sir,' Danizon said. 'I was struck by the coincidence. It's Warrender, Clansel and Warrender, of Lincoln's Inn.'

'So it is,' said Roger tautly. 'Telephone Rachel Warrender and ask her to meet me at the Yard in an hour. You'd better be there, too. I'll be out of here in five minutes, and I'm going over to the Festival Hall, to see the commander.'

'But if you interrupt him at the conference, sir—' Alarm thickened Danizon's voice.

'I'll either be out on my neck or the next deputy commander,' Roger said drily. 'I know.'

In ten minutes he was outside in the Strand, facing a battery of reporters and photographers. A large crowd had gathered, hundreds of people watching the police taking photographs and measurements of the spot where Phillipson had fallen. As West appeared, the crowd surged towards him.

'Just a moment, Super.'

'Hold it.'

'Is it true that you were in the room when Phillipson jumped out of the window?'

'What's it all about, Handsome?'

One man said in a very deep voice, 'Can you give us a statement, sir?'

All this time Roger was pushing his way through the surging mass of onlookers, two constables trying to clear a path for him. Cameras were being held high, photographers were on the roofs of cars, on window ledges, even on one another's shoulders.

'Was it suicide?' one man called.

'Or was he pushed?'

'Just a brief statement, sir,' pleaded the man who had asked before.

Through the crowd Roger could just see the head and shoulders of Detective Constable Ashe. He must be near the car, thought Roger, struggling towards him in the wake of the two constables. At last he reached it, the two policemen as well as Ashe protecting him as he started to get in. Then, standing on the side of the car and supporting himself by the door and a policeman's shoulder, he faced the crowd.

'I'll have a statement of some kind ready at the Yard by seven-thirty,' he called in a clear voice. 'That's a promise.'

There must have been fifty cameras snapping him as he stood there. All questions stopped, he got into the car unhindered, and the crowd drew back, allowing Ashe to drive him away.

Fifteen minutes later he was entering the Royal Festival Hall. This hall, London's musical pride since the 1951 Exhibition, was often used during the day for conferences. On this particular day it was almost filled with policemen from over thirty countries of Europe, including each of the Iron Curtain countries. Roger went to a table marked *Organisation* and spoke to a grey-haired woman whom he vaguely recognised as from the Yard; the Metropolitan Police were responsible for all the arrangements here.

'Good afternoon, Mr. West.'

'Good afternoon. I must speak to Mr. Coppell,' Roger said.

'Oh, no!' she exclaimed. 'The president of the conference is making his closing speech. You can't hear a pin drop in the hall, sir.'

Roger hesitated only for a moment before saying positively, 'Five minutes is the absolute limit I can wait.'

'Oh, but it will be an hour at least! I daren't disturb him.'

'Do you know where Mr. Coppell is?' asked Roger.

'He's about halfway down on the left-hand side of the centre aisle, but the commissioner's with him.'

Roger said, 'Thank you,' and opened a door into the huge auditorium. A man was standing on the huge stage, small, dark-haired, pale-faced, vivid in a single spotlight. He was Karl Schmidt of West Germany, one of the world's great policemen and an orator in German, French and English. The woman was quite right; there was utter stillness and there was magnetism in that clear, only faintly guttural voice.

Roger felt acutely self-conscious, and very glad of the carpeted floor. He passed rows and rows of men, with only here and there a woman, but no one appeared to take the slightest notice of him. He was scanning the heads for Coppell's, which he would recognise—ah! There he was, only one seat off the aisle. Roger drew nearer, and gulped, for the commissioner was in the aisle seat and he could see how intent Trevillion was on the speaker.

...'... and if we are to bring this dreadful wave of crime to an end ...'

Roger summoned up all his courage and bent forward. 'Excuse me, sir,' he whispered, touching Trevillion's arm, 'I must see the commander.'

'What —!' Trevillion ejaculated.

'*Shhh!*' someone hissed.

'*What?*' muttered Trevillion.

Now Coppell had been disturbed, and he turned too. There was just enough light to show Roger's face, as he breathed, 'It's vitally urgent, sir.'

'I'll come,' whispered Coppell.

Roger turned and made his way back, noticed this time by people near the scene of the interruption, aware of many eyes turned towards him. But even so, most eyes were still riveted on the figure on the stage.

'*. . . we have, as we well know, many political problems and social problems but none of us, whatever our ideology, our faith, wants crime on the scale that we now have it. We must find a set of rules to which we can all subscribe; must have co-operation at its closest in the investigation of certain crimes, such as murder for gain . . .*'

Roger went into the foyer, and held the door open. The woman at the table was staring intently; her eyes widened when first Coppell and then the commissioner came out. Roger closed the door quietly, and Coppell said in a growl, 'Your reason had better be good.'

Trevillion was staring at Roger in a puzzled way, not at all censorious or angry; just puzzled. Roger led the way towards a place at the foot of a staircase where no one could come upon them unawares, and overhear what was said.

'Well?' Coppell growled again; whether out of anger or to impress the commissioner, Roger couldn't guess.

'Phillipson of the *Globe* has just committed suicide by throwing himself out of the window of the Allsafe managing director's office,' Roger stated. 'Benjamin Artemeus, of Allsafe, is under arrest on a charge of assisting Phillipson in an attempt to commit grievous bodily harm. Phillipson and Artemeus were conspiring to get control of all the security companies of consequence in the country.

They used me as a pawn to win shareholders' votes. All of these facts can be established from a tape-recording made while I was in Artemeus's office. I have ordered police control of the Allsafe administrative offices and our men are in possession.'

Roger paused, as much for breath as anything else. Neither of the others spoke or moved, and at last he went on, 'I believe the editorial and administrative offices of the *Globe* should be searched forthwith, although it is conceivable that some papers have already been destroyed. I also believe that all the directors and executives of the security companies concerned should be interrogated and their homes searched for incriminating documents. Further, I believe that the law firm of Warrender, Clansel and Warrender is involved, and I think its offices and the homes of its partners should be searched, at once.'

He paused again, and this time Coppell gasped, 'Good God!'

'I did not feel that I could give orders for these raids on my own account,' Roger said. 'We need all available men from the C.I.D.: all officers off duty should, in my opinion, be called in so that a clean sweep can be made tonight. I doubt if any of the suspects will expect such immediate action, but if we wait until tomorrow then any incriminating documents could be burned or otherwise destroyed, while any individuals engaged in the conspiracy could get together to offer false explanations and in some cases might flee the country during the night.' He moistened his lips, but paused only for a moment. 'I hope you will authorise the raids, gentlemen. I believe them to be essential.'

'And Phillipson is *dead*!' said the commissioner, incredulously. 'I know—I knew him well.'

Was he going to be as slow as that in catching up with the situation? Roger wondered desperately.

'We'd better hear that tape-recorder,' Coppell said. 'Is your car outside, Handsome?'

'At the door.'

'Shall we go in that?' Coppell suggested to the commissioner. It was almost a direction and they moved towards the door. 'We can hear the rest of West's story on the way.'

Ashe, talking to a doorman, was suddenly at attention as the three men appeared, and at the car door in giant strides. There was no room for three big men in the back seat, so Roger got into the seat next to Ashe, switched off the two-way radio, and twisted round so that he could face his two seniors. His head was bent because of the low roof, and his side hurt where he had been kicked, but his heart was light because he now knew that he was being taken with utter seriousness. But he still hadn't reached the crux of his belief—his fear.

'Now, proceed,' said the commissioner.

'The tape will establish what I've already said'—Roger went on as if there had been no interruption—'and at least three of our men saw Phillipson throw himself out of the window. I was nearer him than anyone else, but still six or seven feet away. The rest is based largely on conjecture.'

'You mean, the justification for these wholesale raids you want?' asked Coppell.

'On some of the most distinguished men in the country,' Trevillion put in sonorously.

'Yes,' answered Roger, crisply. 'It really turns on the fact that Rachel Warrender came to see me and pleaded with me to find out the truth. She told me that she had been in love with Rapelli, that she had believed in him, but that she now found he had bribed his witnesses. She also told me that her father—Sir Roland Warrender—had begged her not to take the case, and she seemed extremely worried about this—almost as if she suspected his motives. She was in very great distress, both for Rapelli's sake *and* for reasons which might well concern her father.'

He paused, moistening his lips again; his mouth was very dry.

'*Warrender*,' murmured Coppell, '*Phillipson* ...'

Roger's heart and hopes leapt in unison.

'But what has the error of judgment of a young woman solicitor to do with this?' demanded Trevillion.

'I think she feared her father was involved but couldn't bring herself to spy on him or even give direct information,' Roger said slowly. 'I believe she came to give me the vital clue: that her father, one of the most extreme right-wing politicians in Britain, could be involved.'

'With the most extreme right-wing newspaper,' breathed Coppell.

'That's right,' said Roger. Thank God Coppell was police-trained, he thought, and saw the significance of all this way ahead of Trevillion. 'It all began to fit. I was the pawn, as I've said—I had to be the figurehead behind whom the shareholders of Allsafe would rally. And once I had joined them, I was to be built-up by the *Globe* as a victim of the intolerable rigidity of the Yard's policy. I was to be a victim of *your* tyrannical attitude, sir. I was to be the golden boy who could no longer work at the Yard, being blocked at every turn by red tape, officialdom and—no doubt—by governmental control through the Home Office.' He was looking at Trevillion, who frowned slightly at the accusations but made no comment. 'And once I was trapped, once I was the figurehead, once the reputation of the Yard had been effectively smeared and the reputation of the police trampled in the dust, once all the major security forces were merged under one control—'

'They would be in competition with us!' cried Coppell.

In the silence which followed, Ashe took his eyes off the road for a moment and gaped at Roger. A car horn hooted, and he swung the wheel in a moment of alarm, but none of the passengers noticed.

'They might even be in a position to take over now,' Roger said, grimly. 'Most of their staff are ex-Yard and ex-policemen, many of them in their early fifties, even in their late forties. They would have all the makings of an alternative police force.'

'West,' said Trevillion, in a curiously flat voice, 'do you know what you're saying?'

'Yes, sir,' answered Roger, quietly. 'I couldn't understand why they should go to such lengths to discredit me at the Yard and at the same time discredit the Yard itself. But I can see a very likely reason now. And I can also see beyond this to a political crisis, sir. We are in a constant succession of political emergencies. The *Globe* has been campaigning for a businessman's government for years; has even advocated benevolent dictatorship as the way out of our political and economic troubles. Artemeus is right-wing. Sir Roland Warrender has been the rallying point at Westminster for discontent with the present form of government, and there have been some indications that he either sees himself as a leader, or others see him as one—'

'You think there could be an attempt to take over the country,' interrupted Trevillion. He did not raise his voice but spoke as if it were hurtful for him to say such things. 'And you want these raids made to ensure that if there *is* any plot, then it is smashed now, before the ringleaders can escape to plot again. Is that it?'

Roger said simply, 'That is it exactly, sir.'

The commissioner, sitting bolt upright, looked like an image of Buddha. He stared intently into Roger's eyes, and then turned to Coppell. It was a long time before he spoke.

'If I were in absolute control,' he said at last, 'I would call out the armed forces to make these raids. But the point you have made very successfully in the past few weeks is that my methods are not police methods. What do you advise, Commander?'

So now everything was in the hands of the commander, C.I.D. It was up to Coppell, thought Roger grimly, to prove his capacity for dealing with such a desperate situation.

Chapter Twenty

POLICEMAN

Coppell was looking at Roger, not at Trevillion. The car was now in Parliament Square, but none of them glanced up and none appeared to realise the appositeness of this place at this moment—unless Ashe did. He was tense-faced and his hands, usually relaxed, were tight on the wheel.

'I would assign every man we've got, off duty or on, to these raids.' Coppell spoke slowly, weightily. 'I would brief all the divisions, call for help from the City Police, be completely ready to make the raids, while you were placing the known facts before the Home Secretary. And I would be ready to move the moment he approved.'

Roger thought almost desperately: But supposing he wouldn't give the word?

Trevillion frowned.

'I see. Yes. However, supposing the Home Office became entangled in all that red tape which West feels can be such a disadvantage? Supposing I told the Prime Minister —who will be at the Euro-Police Conference tonight—and the Prime Minister called a cabinet meeting and the cabinet ministers dithered?' Trevillion looked at Roger with a wry smile, then turned back to Coppell. 'I'm a naval man, Commander. Often have to take decisions and justify them afterwards. If it's a wrong decision one is in serious trouble, but there isn't time for reference back to

Whitehall when one is under direct enemy attack.' He paused, looked from Coppell to Roger, then back again to Coppell. 'Set the Yard at Action Station, Commander,' he said harshly, 'and move into action the moment you're ready. And don't lose a *second*. Understand?'

Coppell was already leaning forward to switch on the radio. By the time they reached the Yard, men were coming in for instructions and every division had been alerted for a raid or raids which might take all night. The Press was clamouring outside the Yard and cameras clicked again and again.

They went inside.

'What do you have to do now?' Coppell asked Roger.

'I promised the Press a statement at the Back Room at seven-thirty,' Roger said. 'But I'm anxious to interview Rachel Warrender at once.'

'I'll fix the statement. You see the Warrender girl and let me know when you're through,' said Coppell.

'West,' said Trevillion, rubbing his jaw, 'I want you to understand one thing. Whether you're right or whether you're wrong, you've done a remarkable job in a remarkable way. I'm sorry I made it difficult for you.'

He nodded, and moved off.

Coppell cleared his throat.

'Couldn't agree with him more, Handsome. I made it bloody difficult, too. I'm no public relations man. Can never say what I mean to say, if there's a back, I put it up. Early on, I wanted to tell you something but couldn't get it out, you can put my back up, too.' His face was thunderous as he said all this and the shadows seemed to grow darker as he went on, 'I'm going to retire. Only got three months to go. I had to recommend someone to take my place. You. But Trevillion had doubts, thought you were a show-off—and in a way I agree with him. You had me over a barrel. But there was a thing I didn't know.

You shot up high in his opinion when you fought him and me. He *likes* a lone wolf, a man with the guts to make his own decisions. Thought you ought to know.'

He turned and strode off, leaving Roger staring after him in blank astonishment. Roger didn't know how long he had been standing there before he could relax, and then, feeling strangely touched, he went along to his own office. On his desk was a single note, which read:

Miss W. is in my office—been here since 6.49 p.m.

Roger read this two or three times, lit a cigarette, then took out whisky and soda, poured himself a tot, left the bottles out with an empty glass and went to the communicating door.

Rachel was facing him as he opened it. For a moment they stared at each other, while Danizon jumped up from his desk and said in some confusion, 'This is Miss Warrender, sir.'

Slowly she got to her feet and moved like an automaton past Roger and into his office, her face a mask of tragedy and defeat. Roger went to his desk and sat on a corner, gave her a chance to speak, and when she didn't take it, asked, 'Have you heard about Phillipson?'

'Yes.' Her whisper was hardly audible.

'Are you afraid your father might commit suicide, too?'

'No,' she said, a little more strongly. 'He would stand and fight. He will fight.'

'Did you know that there was a plot to set up a rival organisation to the established police forces, one which could take over if there were a coup?'

'No,' she whispered, 'I didn't know—but I feared it. I—I couldn't bear to investigate. So—I came to you. I believed if anyone could find out, you could.'

It would be easy to say that she should have told him, that earlier knowledge might have saved not only trouble but lives, certainly Phillipson's life. But what good pur-

pose could be served? Wouldn't her conscience torment
her enough as the days passed?

'I doubt if I would have seen the truth so quickly if it
hadn't been for you,' he said. 'But even with your help, if
the other security companies hadn't started to gang up on
Allsafe, thus making Phillipson and Artemeus pressure
me too hard, I might not have realised what was going on.'

'And you don't like being pressured,' she remarked.
The faint smile at her lips was a good sign.

'Not in court or out of it! Rachel, *do* you know what
actually happened between Rapelli and Verdi?'

'I didn't,' she answered, 'but I do now. I told you I had
an enquiry agent at work, but in fact this was a member
of the firm's staff. He knew that Mario was a very right-
wing politician who worked for my—my father, whose
activities were nearly treasonable, even to the point of
conspiring with Phillipson and Artemeus to overthrow
the government and establish a new government by thinly
disguised dictatorship.

'This member of the staff knew that Verdi suspected
Mario Rapelli's part in the conspiracy. He and Verdi
used to work together at rallies and demonstrations, but
Verdi discovered they were planning a coup, and he
threatened to tell the police. Mario killed him to keep
him quiet. Maisie had no idea what was going on, but
Fogarty had. And when Hamish Campbell found out, he
switched sides because of *his* right-wing sympathies. They
all panicked,' she added helplessly. 'When you went to
Fogarty's room they thought you would find some
documents and literature there that would give the game
away, and Campbell tried—Well, you know what
followed.'

'It was quite an extravaganza,' Roger said. 'But I am
beginning to understand it. They were so desperate that
they took wild chances.' He frowned. 'Do you know who

killed Maisie, and why?'

'I think I know,' Rachel said. 'After Maisie learnt that Fogarty had killed Smithson she wouldn't have anything more to do with him. I think she was beginning to put two and two together, and they thought she knew more than she actually did. The only person she'd speak to was Rapelli, and I think someone went to her flat pretending to be Rapelli, and attacked her before she had time to find out who he really was.'

'One thing you should know, sir,' Danzion said later. 'They found a section of a thumbprint on the hammer handle, the hammer used to kill Maisie. We shall get him.'

'Check it with Fogarty's,' Roger ordered.

They learned, soon, that it was Fogarty's print.

*   *   *

'So I killed Smithson,' Fogarty said hoarsely. 'And I'd kill you, Rachel Warrender and the whole gang of hypocrites who support the bloody system we live under. We've got to have a change, don't you understand? And we can only get it by revolution.'

'There are some things that make me feel murderous, too,' Roger said, tautly. 'Such as Maisie's death.'

'But I didn't want to kill Maisie,' Fogarty cried. 'She was the mother of my son—sure, she had a son, that's what she always wanted money for, she paid a foster mother to look after the kid. *I didn't want to kill her!*' he cried again. 'But she learned too much, she could have brought disaster on everything and everyone I believe in!'

Roger left him and went to the Yard, where he studied the latest reports on Rapelli. Only this afternoon, since he had looked at the film, was there any reference to Rapelli's political activities. '*He is a member of an extreme right-wing underground group which used the Doon Club as cover.'*

'We should have discovered that earlier,' Roger reproached himself. And it was no consolation to know that he would have come round to it sooner or later.

He went straight from the Yard to Brixton Prison. Soon, Rapelli was brought to see him, and obviously the man had heard something of what had happened. He was edgy, his lips twitched occasionally, he clenched and unclenched his hands.

'I've just come from Fogarty,' Roger said coldly. 'And I know why you attacked Verdi.'

Rapelli said in a hoarse voice, 'Is it true that Phillipson of the *Globe* killed himself?'

'Yes, and it is true that after a study of papers found in his office and in Artemeus's office we know both men were involved in a plot to overthrow the government and impose one on the country. We also know you were involved, that Verdi found out and refused to go along, and—'

'You can guess what you like,' Rapelli interrupted. 'I admit nothing, do you understand? Nothing.'

*　　*　　*

Roger telephoned Rachel Warrender at her Hampstead flat, and told her what he had said to Rapelli. Very slowly she answered, 'It's one thing to be a Fascist, another to be a cold-blooded murderer. But I'll go and see him in the morning, Mr. West.'

'I hoped you would,' said Roger.

'I'm sure you did,' said Rachel in a very emphatic way. 'You're one of the rare human beings who would help his own worst enemy, aren't you? We'll meet again, Mr. West, but just now I would like to thank you for being exactly what you are.'

When he rang off, he sat very still and silent. But he could not sit idle for long. He wanted to be at the hub of the Yard, helping to organise the raids, to be the first to hear the results.

There was an air of hustle and bustle and excitement as the different teams went out, first to the divisions, then to the offices and the houses of the people involved. Soon, more evidence came in of the plot. Documents found in Sir Roland Warrender's safe proved what he had been planning, and Sir Roland admitted everything to a Yard superintendent.

His firm's partners were involved, too, except for Rachel.

So were some of the directors and major shareholders of the *Globe*.

The raid on the *Globe* was a masterly achievement; everyone who knew what Phillipson had planned was charged, but most of the reporting, administrative and machine-room staff were quite unaware that the *Globe* was to have been the voice of rebellion, and they produced the next edition with banner headlines about the story.

By midnight, the raids were nearly all over, key houses and offices were taken over by the police. First the Home Secretary and then the Prime Minister were told, and faced with a *fait accompli*, gave their approval. Two cabinet ministers were on the fringe of the organisation as a political machine, a few members of Parliament had been aware of what Warrender was planning, but none had known of the Allsafe plot. Just after midnight, Roger was still at his desk when Coppell and Trevillion came in.

'All that matters is done for the night,' Coppell said, 'I'll stay and see it through. You go home, Handsome. You need some rest.'

'That's an order,' the commissioner insisted, with a

glint in his eyes.

Yes, it was time to go home; time to see Janet.

He had telephoned home and talked to Martin, telling him he would be late, asking him to tell Janet not to sit up, but Janet might have ignored that, and be waiting. What was she thinking? As far as she knew he had been offered an ideal job and not told her and not accepted it. He drove to Bell Street, slowly, and went right into the garage. The living room lights were on, so Janet hadn't gone to bed. Oh, well. As he opened the kitchen door he heard the television, and was startled. Only rarely, and usually for political occasions, was there television after midnight. He reached the door and looked in. Both the boys and Janet sat round the screen, and there was no commentary, just some street scenes—Strand scenes. There was a picture of a man on the pavement—Phillipson! So a camera had been there that early. There were shots of the ambulance, of Phillipson being lifted in, of more police cars arriving, then, suddenly, pictures of a seething crowd of people.

'There he is!' cried Janet.

'Good old Pop!' chortled Richard.

'*Hush!*' breathed Scoop.

The camera followed him, Roger, as he pushed and the police pushed and at last he was at the car. Slowly he turned to face the crowd, and a remarkable silence fell upon the people. He looked round, and, watching, he was satisfied with his poise. His voice came from the television, as Janet said with a choky kind of emotion, 'Oh, he's wonderful!'

'*I'll have a statement of some kind ready at the Yard by seven-thirty. That's a promise.*'

'Do you know,' Scoop said, 'I've never yet known Dad break a promise?'

'*Hush!*' breathed Richard.

There was a swift change of scene to the news room at Scotland Yard, in fact a conference room which was jammed tight with people. The commentator used as few words as he could as first Coppell and then the commissioner spoke.

'We can't and won't answer any questions,' Trevillion said, 'but Commander Coppell has a statement which we have both signed. Copies will be available as you leave the room. *Harrumph!* Commander.'

The camera switched to Coppell's face, his deepset eyes, his heavy jaw. He read the statement slowly, almost at dictation speed.

'A series of raids on professional, commercial and (one) newspaper building have been and are being made by officers of the Metropolitan Police Force in conjunction with the City of London Police Force this evening. Raids have been and are being carried out also on private homes. A number of arrests have already been made and others are pending. The charge in each case is that of conspiring against the State.

'This is only a preliminary statement. No others will be issued tonight and no questions will be answered. It can be stated, however, that these raids followed the death by suicide of the editor of the *Globe*, and that among those arrested are Sir Roland Warrender, M.P., Benjamin Artemeus of the Allsafe Security Company, and members of the boards of both of these as well as other companies and partnerships.

'We are of the opinion that it should be stated that these raids, and the arrests of individuals inimical to the state, were made at the instigation of Chief Superintendent Roger West. Further, it should be stated that among those charged is Miss Gwendoline Ferrow, secretary to the undersigned, Commander Coppell.'

The picture faded.

Coppell's bitchy secretary! Roger gasped inwardly. So *that* was how so much information had been leaked.

Martin got up slowly and moved to the screen and switched off. Then he saw Roger. Showing no sign that he had done so, he went across to Janet, by whom Richard was already sitting. With a gleam in his eyes, he asked,

'Good thing he didn't take that job, isn't it, Mum?'

'Yes,' Janet said huskily. 'Yes, it is. Not that anything would ever make him resign from the Force until he's compelled to by old age. It's his life. I *do* know, boys. Try —try to make him understand. I do. I tried to get him this afternoon, I wanted to tell him that this man Artemeus was obviously trying to make me persuade him! But nothing would have made me. I wanted to try to make him understand that I know he would hate to work for Allsafe, that he mustn't do it for me.' She paused, looked from one son to the other, and then asked in a pleading voice, 'Do you think, after all I've said in the past, that he will believe me?'

Martin looked down on her solemnly, then glanced over her head at Roger, and said, 'Why don't you ask him?'

Janet sprang up and spun round. Roger moved towards her. He could never know the brilliance in his eyes, the glow, the satisfaction which shone in his face.

'Come on, Fish,' said Martin-called-Scoopy. 'This is no place for little boys.'